PAUL TEMPLE AND THE MARGO MYSTERY

Francis Henry Durbridge was born in Hull, Yorkshire, in 1912 and was educated at Bradford Grammar School. He was encouraged at an early age to write by his English teacher and went on to read English at Birmingham University. At the age of twenty one he sold a play to the BBC and continued to write following his graduation whilst working as a stockbroker's clerk.

In 1938, he created the character Paul Temple, a crime novelist and detective. Many others followed and they were hugely successful until the last of the series was completed in 1968. In 1969, the Paul Temple series was adapted for television and four of the adventures prior to this, had been adapted for cinema, albeit with less success than radio and TV. Francis Durbridge also wrote for the stage and continued doing so up until 1991, when *Sweet Revenge* was completed. Additionally, he wrote over twenty other well received novels, most of which were on the general subject of crime. The last, *Fatal Encounter*, was published after his death in 1998.

Also in this series

FRANCIS DURBRIDGE

Paul Temple and the Margo Mystery

COLLINS
CRIME
CLUB

COLLINS CRIME CLUB

An imprint of HarperCollins*Publishers*
1 London Bridge Street
London SE1 9GF
www.harpercollins.co.uk

This paperback edition 2015

First published in Great Britain by
Hodder & Stoughton 1986

Copyright © Francis Durbridge 1986

Francis Durbridge has asserted his right under the Copyright,
Designs and Patents Act, 1988 to be identified as the author of this work

A catalogue record for this book is
available from the British Library

ISBN 978-0-00-812576-9

Set in Sabon by Born Group using Atomik ePublisher from Easypress

Printed and bound in Great Britain

CHAPTER I

The Coat

Thanks to a cab driver with the nerve of a Grand Prix racer Paul Temple caught the morning flight from New York to London by the skin of his teeth. As a Concorde passenger he received VIP treatment and was hustled through the departure formalities. Less than an hour after leaving his hotel on Fifth Avenue he was in his window seat watching John F. Kennedy Airport drop rapidly away as Concorde soared towards her cruising height. Some other passengers must have cut things even finer, for the seat beside him had remained empty.

He listened patiently to the stewardess going through the familiar demonstration of the emergency equipment, waiting for the illuminated sign to be switched off so that he could unfasten his safety belt. As the Captain finished his reassuring announcement he made his way forward to put through the telephone call to London which he had booked on boarding.

One of the stewardesses, who had put on her in-flight overall, stood aside to let him pass. Her smile was not purely automatic. It was a pleasure to see someone whose style matched that of the aircraft. Temple, with his well-cut clothes, tall build and clean-cut features looked as British as the Rolls-Royce engines that were driving them through the air faster than a bullet leaving a rifle.

Temple's decision to return home had been made last thing the evening before and his wife Steve would need some warning that he would be arriving two days early.

When he returned to his seat he found that a youngish man had ensconced himself in the empty place. He smiled apologetically and swung his knees sideways to let Temple pass.

'I hope you don't mind. I saw that this seat was empty.' The accent was American, but suggestive of Boston rather than the Bronx.

'Not at all,' Temple said, removing *The New York Times* from his seat before he sat down. 'I thought someone must have missed the plane.'

'Oh, I have a seat further back. I flew in from California overnight and had a couple of hours' wait at Kennedy. Nice to think we'll be in London just about the same time as we left New York. Your Concorde sure is a fantastic aircraft.'

'Yes, and this new telephone link by satellite is a great advantage. I've just been talking to my wife.'

'Mrs Temple doesn't come on these trips with you?' The man laughed when he saw Temple's surprise. 'You don't remember me? My name's Langdon. Mike Langdon. We met in Hollywood, Mr Temple.'

'Did we?' Temple turned to look at his neighbour more closely. He was wearing a lightweight suit and his confident manner was that of a hard-thrusting businessman who does not mind cutting a few corners to achieve his targets. His dark curly hair was cut close to his head and he must have found time to shave during his wait at Kennedy, for his cheeks were smooth. Temple could often tell as much about a person from his hands as from his facial features, but Langdon held his hands firmly folded in his lap as if determined to keep them strictly under control.

'You don't remember?'

'I'm sorry.' Langdon was holding his gaze. 'I've met so many people during these past weeks—'

'Yes, of course.' Langdon smiled, remembering some scene that Temple had forgotten. 'I was at that party the film people gave you – me and about two hundred others.'

'Yes.' Temple smiled in reply. 'That was quite a party, wasn't it?'

'It sure was.'

'Are you in the film business, Mr Langdon?'

'No.' Langdon glanced down to adjust the cuffs of his shirt, making sure that they protruded just one quarter of an inch. 'I'm with a publishing firm in New York, Talbot and Ryder. It's only a small outfit, but we do very nicely. I'm sorry we don't have your books on our list, Mr Temple, but I guess we can't afford the advances the big boys put up. How did the lecture tour go?'

'Oh, very well, thank you, but it was a bit wearing at times.'

'I'll bet!' Langdon agreed emphatically. 'Our authors hate 'em. Still, they're first-rate publicity.'

The conversation was interrupted as two stewardesses came along with the Concorde ration of vintage champagne. Langdon shook his head and insisted on a Scotch on the rocks.

'Is this your first trip to Europe?' Temple enquired, savouring his Veuve Clicquot. The aircraft had climbed through cloud and was now flying over a cotton-wool landscape under blue skies.

'No. I've been over many times before. I was in Paris two weeks ago.' Langdon turned sideways in his seat, swirling the ice round in his glass. Temple sensed that he was now about to learn why Langdon had wanted to sit beside him. 'Mr Temple, have you heard of a young man called Tony Wyman?'

'No, I don't think so. Should I have done?'

'Well, I understand he's fairly well-known in your country. He's a pop singer.'

'Tony Wyman?' Temple shook his head. 'Is he a friend of yours?'

'No.' Langdon gave a short laugh. 'And I doubt whether he'll turn out to be one, either.' He eased a little closer and leant his forearm on the armrest between them. 'Mr Temple, I've got quite a problem on my hands and I'd sure like to talk about it. Is that okay by you?'

'Why, yes.' Temple, who was used to this kind of approach, smiled wryly. 'Go ahead.'

'About two years ago my firm was taken over by an Englishman called George Kelburn. If you don't know Kelburn personally, you've probably read about him.'

'Yes, I've heard of Kelburn. He's a north-country chap, reputed to be worth millions.'

'That's right. Well, when Kelburn took our firm over he made me the Number One boy. He's a blunt, ruthless sort of guy, but we've always got on well together.'

Temple thought Langdon looked as if he was well able to handle a blunt, ruthless sort of guy.

'He'd be a good deal older than you?'

'Yes, he's about sixty, maybe sixty-two or three. I'm not sure.'

Langdon screwed his eyes up against a sudden dazzle. As the plane banked the sunlight was reflected into the cabin off its gleaming wing.

'Go on, Mr Langdon,' Temple prompted.

'Well, Kelburn's first wife died some years ago and he married again – a woman a lot younger than himself. He has a daughter, Julia, by his first wife. Julia's twenty-one – young, attractive and hopelessly spoilt.'

'Not an unusual story,' said Temple with a smile.

'No, I suppose not, but – well, to cut a long story short, Julia's got herself tangled up with this night-club singer, Tony Wyman, and she's told her father that she intends to marry the guy.'

'And Kelburn's against it?'

'Against it?' Langdon looked deadly serious. 'Kelburn's going to stop that marriage if it's the last thing he does.'

'Yes, but – how do you fit into all this, Mr Langdon? If you're just a business associate of Kelburn's . . .'

'That's just the point,' Langdon interrupted, with exasperation. 'I don't fit into it! But Kelburn sent me an SOS, and there was nothing I could do about it.'

'You mean, he wants you to try and influence her to . . .'

'Exactly! Julia and I have always got on well together, so he wants me to talk to the kid and try to persuade her to throw the boyfriend over.'

'Do you think you've got much chance?'

'None.' Langdon shook his head morosely. 'I've got no special influence with her, and according to all accounts she's nuts about this Tony Wyman.'

'You seem to be in quite a spot.'

'You can say that again! Well, you're used to other people's troubles, Mr Temple! What would you do if you were in my shoes?'

Temple had warmed to Langdon, whose frank helplessness was rather disarming. The problem was a pleasantly banal one, after the murders and other vicious crimes which he was usually called on to solve. 'Frankly, I don't know what I'd do.'

'If I refuse to help Kelburn he'll put me on the spot businesswise – there's no doubt about that, I know Kelburn. On the other hand, if I get mixed up in it and make a mess of things, which is more than likely, it isn't going to do me any good either.'

A stewardess was moving back along the cabin, collecting the empty glasses. Temple finished his champagne and placed the glass on the folding table ready for her.

'And how does Kelburn's wife react to all this?'

'Oh, Laura takes the point of view that Julia's twenty-one and she'll do what she likes, anyway.'

'I see.'

'This whole business has turned up at a very awkward moment, so far as I'm concerned. I've had a hectic time just lately – been in ten countries in two months, and right now I'm ready for a holiday, not a first-class family squabble.'

'Well, there's no point in anticipating trouble, Mr Langdon,' Temple told him reassuringly. 'Perhaps when you get to London you'll find the situation has straightened itself out.'

'I certainly hope so.'

'Anyway, I'm in the 'phone book. If you feel I can help you at any time, give me a ring.'

'Well, now, that's very kind of you, Mr Temple.' Obviously delighted, Langdon stretched out his free hand and insisted on shaking Temple's. 'I do appreciate it, sir. I certainly do!'

The stewardess leant across him to pick up Temple's glass. 'Will you be returning to your seat, sir?' she enquired, 'or remaining here? We shall shortly be serving lunch.'

'Oh, I'd better get back to my own seat,' Langdon said, rising. 'And thanks again, Mr Temple. I may take you up on that offer.'

Steve returned to the flat at about two thirty after lunching in the West End. The flat always seemed so empty when Temple was away, and she began to wish she had accepted her friend's invitation to go and see the new exhibition at the Hayward Gallery. She went into the bedroom and unpacked the new dress she had bought. She wanted to surprise Paul with something really smart when he came back from his lecture tour. As she held it against herself and studied the effect in the long mirror she decided that a new pair of shoes and a handbag were essential to match it. Rather than hide it away in the long cupboard, she hung it on the back of the door where she could see it and wandered aimlessly into the sitting-room.

The trees in Eaton Square were beginning to bud and the city birds had already started to prophesy spring. A couple of the early daffodils she had bought to brighten the place up had begun to wilt. She had picked them out of the vase and was throwing them into the waste-paper basket when Charlie came in. He was carrying a cup on a tray.

'Thought you might like a cup of coffee.'

'Oh, thank you, Charlie. Just put it down on the table.'

Charlie was the Temples' driver, cook, odd-job man and watchdog. His familiarity sometimes verged on impertinence but he was loyal and faithful as a spaniel. The forty-year-old Cockney had been with them for more years than any of them cared to remember and had his own sitting-room and bedroom beyond a door whose threshold neither Paul nor Steve would have presumed to cross. The only disadvantage about Charlie was his unfortunate lack of dress sense. Steve tried not to show her disapproval of the lumberjack shirt and the too tight check trousers.

'What time is it, Charlie?'

'Just gone 'arf past two,' said Charlie, setting the cup and saucer down on a low table. 'Cream's in it already but I didn't put any sugar, like you said.'

'Only half past two. How slowly the days go! I thought it was later than that. In New York it must be nine thirty.'

Charlie paused, knowing that she needed company. 'Yes, I suppose it will. Five hours back. Do you think Mr Temple will have had breakfast yet?'

'Well, I should hope so, Charlie. He promised to get through his schedule as quickly as possible.'

'When are you expecting him back, Mrs Temple?'

'Some time next week, if all goes well.'

Charlie stared sympathetically at her dejected face. 'I'll bet you'll be glad.'

'That's the understatement of the year. It seems as if he's been away for months.'

'Four weeks and a day.' Charlie saw the discarded daffodils in the waste-paper basket and went over to pick them up. 'You know, I can't understand why you didn't go with him. You usually—'

'Have you ever been to America on a lecture tour, Charlie?'

'No,' Charlie admitted, after a moment's thought. 'Can't say as I 'ave.'

'Twenty-two towns in four weeks. That's not my idea of –' She stopped as the telephone in the hall began to ring. 'Oh, see who that is, Charlie, will you? If it's those people who want to clean our carpets say I'm not in.'

She heard Charlie pick up the telephone and give the number. Almost at once he called: 'Mrs Temple! Quick! It's Mr Temple.'

Steve ran to seize the receiver from him. 'Paul, darling! Where are you?'

'About thirty thousand feet over the east coast of Canada. I'm on Concorde.'

'But Paul, how on earth—? I didn't know you could—'

'Listen, Steve. How are you?'

'I'm fine. Looking forward to next week.'

'I've got news for you. I've finished my tour early and I'm on my way back. We're due to land at London Airport at seven fifteen.'

'Oh, *that* Concorde! But how are you able to 'phone me? The line's so clear.'

'Don't worry about that. Now, you've got the message? I'll be home tonight.'

'Seven fifteen at London Airport. Bet your sweet life I'll be there!'

'There's no need to meet me, darling. I can take a taxi.'

'Just you try and stop me. What's the flight number?'

'Just ask for Concorde, Terminal Three. Goodbye, Steve. See you at Heathrow.'

Charlie was alone in the flat at a quarter to eight when the telephone rang. He came out of the kitchen, wiping his hands on the faded blue and white housemaid's apron he always wore when he was cooking.

'Mr Temple's residence.'

'Is that you, Charlie?'

'Mr Temple! Where are you?'

'I'm at the airport. Is Mrs Temple with you?'

'Why no! I thought she'd be with you, Mr Temple. She left here two hours ago.'

'Did she take the car?'

'Yes—the MG Metro.'

'You're sure she knew the time and place?'

'Yes, she knew the time and place all right. She's been talking about nothing else all afternoon.'

'I see.' Temple's tone was worried. 'Did she say whether she had any calls to make?'

'No, but I don't think she had.' Charlie was certain that Steve had had no other thought in her mind except to meet her husband. 'I hope there hasn't been an accident . . .'

'Yes, I hope so too, Charlie,' Temple said gravely. 'I'll see you later.'

'Very good, sir.' Unusually subdued, Charlie replaced the receiver.

The homecoming dinner prepared with such care by Charlie had proved to be wasted effort. On arriving back at the flat Temple had declared himself unable to swallow a mouthful after the meal he had eaten on Concorde, and five hours after she had left for the airport there was still neither sight nor sound of Steve. Charlie had salvaged what he could and stored it away in the deep-freeze for some future occasion. He was in his bed-sitter watching the TV commercials that preceded the ten o'clock news when there came a long ring on the doorbell followed by an authoritative rat-tat-tat on the knocker.

Charlie, divested of his apron and wearing a jacket which noticeably failed to match his trousers, went to open it. Of the two men standing on the landing outside he was already familiar with one. Sir Graham Forbes was the kind of Englishman who had been formed by the successive processes of school, university, military service and public office. With his broad shoulders, bristling grey moustache, bushy eyebrows and a certain aura of unshakable confidence he was still impressive enough to attract the glances of women.

'Good evening, Charlie,' he said, as one greeting an old friend.

'Good evening, sir. Mr Temple's expecting you.'

'Any news?' Sir Graham asked, as he stepped into the hall.

'No, sir. I'm afraid not.'

The heavily built man with Forbes was at least fifteen years younger and of a very different type. He was soberly dressed with a plain tie and well-polished black shoes. Charlie, who was at heart a downright snob, could see at a glance that he had made his way in the world by his own unaided efforts, assisted by no advantages of family or money. Charlie was not endeared by the way those hard eyes swept over him, missing not a detail of his dress and physical features. He had the uncomfortable feeling that he was being checked against some rogues' gallery that the police officer carried in a computer-like mind.

'In here, Sir Graham,' he said, fussing over the taller man and ignoring the other. 'Mr Temple's in the sitting-room.'

Temple, who had also been watching the ten o'clock ITV news, half expecting to hear that there had been some horrific pile-up on the M4 between London and Heathrow, switched the set off and came across the room to meet his visitors.

'Come in, Sir Graham. It's very kind of you to come at such short notice.'

'My dear fellow, I'd have got here sooner only I was already half-way home from my club when your message came through. And when Steve is concerned—'

'I understand there's no news, Mr Temple,' the police officer said, anxious to make the point that he too had forsaken hearth and home to accompany Sir Graham.

Temple turned towards him and the eyes of the two men met with mutual appraisal and respect. Raine, of course, had known Temple's reputation as a criminologist as well as an author, even before the briefing Forbes had given him in the car.

'No, I'm afraid not.'

'This is Superintendent Raine, Temple.' Forbes put a friendly hand on the Scotland Yard man's shoulder. 'I don't think you've met before.'

'No, I don't think we have. Though I read about your handling of the Belgrave Square siege.' The two men shook hands, still measuring each other with their eyes. Temple assessed Raine as thorough and methodical but perhaps a little unimaginative. 'How do you do, Superintendent.'

'Pleased to meet you, Mr Temple.'

'Sit down and I'll get you a drink.'

'No, no. Don't worry about drinks.' Forbes brushed the offer aside, to Raine's evident disappointment. 'Temple, tell me, have you checked the hospitals?'

'I've checked every hospital within thirty miles of the airport,' Temple said wearily. 'It took me the whole evening.'

Raine had seated himself on the front edge of one of the easy chairs. 'I understand you found Mrs Temple's car?'

'Yes, Superintendent. It was in the car park at the airport. The attendant remembered her arriving – about half an hour before my plane was due. She'd left her coat in the back of the car, so she couldn't have intended to go much further than the lounge, or maybe the restaurant.'

'I take it Mrs Temple didn't leave a note for you, sir, or anything which might . . .'

'No. I've been through the place pretty thoroughly, and apart from a telephone message there's nothing – absolutely nothing.'

Forbes, who had taken up his customary position in front of the fireplace with legs astride, asked: 'What was the telephone message?'

'It was on the pad upstairs. It simply said: "Tell P." – which is obviously me – "about L."'

'Who's L, Temple?'

'I don't know. But I don't think it's important, Sir Graham. According to Charlie, the message was written several days ago.'

'Well, I'm sorry, Mr Temple,' Raine commented in his deliberate way, 'but it looks as if we shall have to face the facts. The only explanation I can see is that your wife's been waylaid by someone. Now the question is . . .'

He was interrupted by the ringing of the telephone out in the hall. Temple exchanged a quick glance of hope with Forbes before he went out to pick the receiver up.

'Hello?'

He could hear the bleep-bleep, indicating that the call was coming from a pay 'phone. There was a clunk as a coin was pushed into the slot. Then Temple heard a man's voice, muffled but obviously in the same call-box.

'All right. Go ahead. Talk to him now . . .'

'Hello!' Temple repeated impatiently. 'Hello, who is that?'

There was a pause, and then: 'Is that you, Paul?' The woman's voice was so weak that he hardly recognised it as Steve's.

'Steve! Is that you, Steve?'

'Paul, can you hear me?'

He could tell from her voice that she was very frightened. 'Steve, where are you?'

'Don't worry, dear.' Scared though she was, she was trying to reassure him. 'There's nothing to worry about . . .'

13

'Yes, but Steve,' Temple cut in, unable to mask his impatience, 'where are you speaking from?'

'I'm . . . perfectly all right . . .'

'Steve, listen!' Temple was gripping the receiver. 'There was a man on the 'phone, I heard his voice . . . Who was it?'

'Paul, don't try and . . .' Steve's voice was fading, as if someone were pulling the receiver away from her.

'Darling, please tell me . . . Where are you?'

'Oh, Paul . . .' The cry was barely audible. Before Temple could speak again the maddening bleep-bleep had started once more.

'Oh, my God!'

'What's happened?'

Temple looked round to find Raine at his shoulder. 'The line's gone dead.'

'Replace the receiver, Mr Temple – in case she rings back.'

Temple realised that he was still trying to squeeze some response out of the telephone. With deliberate control he replaced it on the cradle.

Forbes had come to the doorway of the sitting-room to listen to Temple's side of the brief conversation. 'You said something about a man, Temple. Was there someone with Steve?'

'Yes. I heard a voice just as I picked up the 'phone. It sounded as if someone was in the call-box with her and was forcing her to . . .'

The 'phone shrilled and Temple scooped it up with one quick movement.

'Take it easy, Temple,' Forbes cautioned.

Temple put a finger into his free ear. 'Hello?'

'Paul—' Steve's voice was a little stronger, but she was still tense.

'Steve,' Temple said, speaking slowly and deliberately but with all the urgency he could muster. 'Where are you calling from?'

'I don't know the number.'

'Darling,' he told her very gently, 'look at the dial.'

'It's a call-box.'

'Well, where is it?'

'Paul, I'm trying to concentrate,' she was evidently dazed and confused, 'but somehow I can't—'

He asked: 'Is there anyone with you?'

'No. Not now, darling.'

'Well,' he tried again, still as if coaxing a frightened child, 'where is the telephone box, Steve?'

'It's at Euston. Just inside the station.' She was near to tears and her voice was beginning to break. 'Please come and fetch me, darling. I'll wait for you in the station near the bookstall.'

'I'll be there in ten minutes!' This time Temple rammed the receiver down on the cradle. His face was grey as he turned to Forbes and Raine. 'She's at Euston Station.'

'Right! Come on, Temple!' Forbes was already heading for the front door. Raine started to follow, but the older man put a finger to stop him and nodded at the telephone.

'Get through to the Yard. Warn all cars in the area but tell them to stay clear of the station. Follow as soon as you can. We'll see you at Euston.'

Knowing that Raine would have no problem with transport, Forbes commandeered the police car waiting down in Eaton Square. The superintendent had chosen as his personal driver a young constable who had passed out of the Police Driving School at Hendon with a Class A. Authorised to use the blue light and siren he made his tyres squeal as he careered round Belgrave Square. The carousel of traffic at Hyde Park Corner yielded to the white police Rover as it squirmed between taxis, buses and private cars. On the Hyde Park ring road they touched a hundred miles an hour and the houses along Park Lane flashed past in a blur. An obstinate Daimler limousine blocked them for a long ten seconds at Marble Arch and received a horn-blasting that sent him rabbiting on to the pavement. As the Rover sped along the Marylebone Road, Forbes and Temple were thrown from side to side when their driver swerved round the slow-moving vehicles, sometimes cutting boldly across to the wrong side of the road and forcing the oncoming traffic to give way to him.

A quarter of a mile from Euston Forbes called out: 'Cut the siren now, Newton.'

Temple glanced at his watch. He had automatically checked the time of Steve's call. It looked as if he was going to keep his promise of being at the station within ten minutes. As if in confirmation the clock of the church across the road began to chime the quarters. Raine's driver braked and swung in through the entrance reserved for buses, slowing behind a Number 14 as it circled the memorial to London and North Eastern Railway personnel killed in the 1914–18 war. Temple, all his senses at full stretch, noted the four statuesque figures guarding it, heads bent over, hands folded on their reversed rifles – an attitude of permanent mourning.

'Well done,' Forbes told the driver, as he deposited them at the kerb. 'Wait for us here.'

Outpacing the passengers who had alighted from the bus, Forbes and Temple hurried across the broad, almost deserted forecourt, past the statue of Robert Stephenson and through the glass doors into the main hall. Both men were wary and watchful. There seemed no good reason why Steve should be kidnapped and then released after only five hours without some sort of pay-off. She could still be in grave danger. At this time of night the bookshop at the east side of the main hall was closed and only a lone vendor of newspapers was doing business.

Temple shook his head. 'She's not here.'

The loudspeakers boomed out some announcement about a train shortly due to depart for Edinburgh. The panels on the indicator-board flapped as a new set of departure times was rung up. From one of the platforms a posse of travellers just in from the North spilled out, dazedly lugging suitcases.

'Is there another bookstall?' Forbes was turning his head this way and that, searching for a slim woman in a blue suit. Charlie had told them what Steve was wearing when she'd set off for the airport.

'There may be.' Temple had started across the spacious hall, his eyes checking the entrances to the bars, restaurants, information desks. People were still crowding up and down the moving staircases leading to the Underground. Half a dozen skinheads were sitting disconsolately in front of the marble plaque commemorating the opening of the new station by Queen Elizabeth II on 14 October 1968. But no sign of Steve.

He stared at the flower-sellers packing up what was left of their stock. The bunches of spring daffodils reminded him vividly of her. So often he had bought her a huge bunch on his way home. Then suddenly, he knew what had happened.

'Sir Graham, you wait here. It's just a thought, but—'

Temple quickly located the sign pointing to the ladies cloakroom. Dazed and scared as she was, Steve would still have been thinking about her appearance. It would be just like her to believe she had time for a quick check-up in front of a mirror. He had entered the opening of the passageway that led to the toilets and was bracing himself to invade the women's domain when he saw a figure in a blue suit coming out through the door. Three seconds later they were in each other's arms.

'Steve!'

'Paul!'

She was almost sobbing with relief. He held her away from him for a moment.

'Darling, you said by the bookstall.'

'Yes, I know. But I knew my face looked awful and I never thought you'd get here so quickly.'

'Well—' Temple let out a long sigh. 'Thank God we've found you.'

Forbes had come striding over from the flower stall. 'Are you all right, Steve?'

'Yes, Sir Graham.' Steve managed a little smile. 'I'm just – a little tired, that's all.'

'What happened?' Temple asked. 'How did you come to be here? Who was that man whose voice I heard?'

'Paul, I'm confused . . . and frightened . . . I hardly know . . .'

'Wait a moment, Temple,' Forbes said in a low voice, his eyes on Steve's trembling hands and nervously restless glance. 'I think we'd better get her home and let a doctor see her before we start asking too many questions.'

'You know, Temple, this really is an extraordinary affair.' Sir Graham Forbes put the glass of whisky Temple had given him on the table beside his chair. 'I've never come across a case quite like it before. No ransom – no mysterious notes – no threats – no blackmail. Nothing.'

'And no motive either, sir,' added Raine, who had opted for a glass of lager, 'so far as we can see.'

The hands of the clock on the mantelpiece of the Temples' sitting-room had moved round to twenty past eleven. More soberly than on the outward journey Raine's driver had brought Steve, Forbes and Temple back to Eaton Square. Temple had been lucky to find the partner of their own doctor at home and he had come round at once. The three men were having a drink while they waited for him to pronounce her fit for questioning.

'They must have had a motive!' Temple exclaimed. He was pacing restlessly up and down the room. 'Whoever they are, they must have had a reason for picking Steve up like that!'

'I agree, Temple. But what was the reason? After all, it isn't as if you're mixed up in a case at the moment, or even helping us over . . .'

Forbes was interrupted by the door opening. Dr McCarthy put his head round it. 'May I come in?'

He was a small, competent but slightly self-effacing man with a balding head and prominent ears. He wore rimless glasses and carried the regulation leather bag.

'Yes, of course, Doctor. What's the verdict?'

'Nothing to worry about – nothing at all.' The doctor ventured a little further into the room. 'But there's no doubt Mrs Temple has had quite a shock, and, in my opinion, she's either been drugged or even possibly hypnotised.'

'Hypnotised!' Temple echoed incredulously.

'However, the main thing is, there's nothing for you to worry about, Mr Temple. What your wife needs now is rest, and plenty of it! I've given her a sedative; she'll probably sleep most of tomorrow morning.'

'Thank you, Doctor.'

'I'll look in during the afternoon, or give you a ring tomorrow evening.'

'Thank you,' Temple said again, and moved towards the door to see him out.

But Dr McCarthy had picked up the purposeful and expectant atmosphere in the room. He peered sternly at Raine through his small lenses. 'And, Superintendent . . .'

'Yes, Doctor?'

'My patient can't answer any questions – not at the moment, at any rate.'

Raine nodded, accepting the ban with resignation. 'Very well, Doctor.'

'So hold your horses until tomorrow.' McCarthy turned to Temple, who was standing waiting by the door. 'And that goes for you too, Mr Temple.'

When Steve woke she did not immediately open her eyes, afraid that she might see again the walls of the small room where she had been held prisoner. But the sound of music was reassuring and she dared to raise her eyelids. With relief she saw that she was in her own bedroom. Though it was darkened she could identify the familiar objects of everyday life.

'Paul . . . What are you doing sitting over there?'

'I'm listening to the radio and watching you, darling.'

'Well, what time is it?'

'What time do you think?' Temple asked, smiling.

'Oh, I don't know.' Steve sat up in bed, stretched her arms and yawned. 'The sun's shining so it must be morning.'

'It's a quarter past five.'

'A quarter past five? In the afternoon?'

'Yes, darling. You've had quite a nice little nap.'

'How long have I actually been . . .?'

'Since eleven o'clock last night.' Temple put the paper down and came over to the bed. 'The doctor gave you a sedative.'

'Good heavens! You shouldn't have let me sleep like this! Oh, Paul – you look wonderful! How lovely to see you again!' She reached out towards him as he bent down to kiss her. 'Did you have a nice trip?'

'Yes, I did. But it's the last trip I'm making without you, Steve.'

'You can say that again!' She laughed and slid luxuriously back under the bedclothes. There was more colour in her cheeks than the night before but she had dark shadows under her eyes.

'How do you feel?'

'I'm perfectly all right now. There's no need to look so anxious.'

He sat down on the edge of the bed. She put out a hand to grasp his. 'Do you feel well enough to talk?'

'Yes, of course.'

'What happened yesterday, Steve?'

'Well, now – let me think . . .' Her eyes clouded as she stared at the half-drawn curtains. 'I'm not sure where to begin . . .'

'Suppose we begin at the very beginning. You set out to meet me at the airport, just as you planned . . .'

'Yes, that's right. I arrived there with plenty of time to spare, and parked the car. A man in uniform, one of the airport officials, came up to me. He checked the number of my car, and asked if I was Mrs Temple. He told me your plane had arrived ahead of schedule and you were waiting for me in the Concorde Lounge.'

'Would you recognise this man again?'

'I doubt it.' She shook her head. 'He asked me to follow him to another car just outside the car park. I thought he was taking me to another building some distance away. In the back of the car was a woman wearing air hostess's uniform. I sat beside her and the man climbed into the driving seat

21

and we drove off. We'd been going for about a minute when the woman suddenly pushed a pad over my face and I felt a jab in my right arm. I'm afraid I don't remember anything else – about the journey, I mean. When I came to I was in a darkened room. I felt absolutely awful. Everything was going round and I wanted to be sick. After a while a man came into the room and gave me a drink. I don't know what it was, but it certainly made me feel better.'

'Was this man the phoney airport official?'

'I couldn't see him very well, but I don't think he was. For one thing, his voice sounded different.'

'And what did he say?'

'He said there was nothing to worry about – that I wasn't in any danger and later on they'd be releasing me.'

'Did you ask why they'd kidnapped you?'

'Yes, and he said: "We did it as a warning, and to prove that it was possible, Mrs Temple." '

She felt his grip on her hand tighten, saw the line of his mouth harden.

'Go on, Steve.'

'Well, I was left alone for ages after that. It must have been two or three hours later before another man came into the room. I think this was the man at the airport; he was about the same height and he sounded rather like him.'

'But you're not sure?' he said sharply.

'No, Paul, I can't be a hundred per cent sure. Anyway, this man also assured me that there was nothing to worry about and that they were going to send me home. About half an hour later they drove me down to Euston and allowed me to make the telephone call.'

'But didn't they give you any idea what this was all about – why they'd abducted you?'

'Not the slightest. Don't you know, Paul?'

'I haven't a clue. I'm not investigating a case at the moment. I'm not mixed up in anything – you know that, Steve.'

'If only I could remember more details . . . What the people looked like . . .'

'Don't worry about it, darling.' He released her hand and stood up. 'You're all right, that's the main thing.'

'Yes, well – you must have been pretty worried.'

'Oh, not really, darling.' He kept his expression dead-pan. 'I just went berserk.'

Steve laughed, watching him affectionately as he moved towards the hanging cupboard that filled one whole wall.

'By the way, I put your new coat in the wardrobe.'

'My coat?'

'Yes. We found it in the back of the car when we collected it from the airport.'

'But I didn't take a coat with me,' Steve said, puzzled.

'Yes, you did, darling. Here it is.' Temple slid the white door back on its runners, reached inside and took out an overcoat on a hanger.

He held the coat up for her to see. It was in classic style, of fawn cashmere, with a tie-belt and sleeves trimmed with leather buttons. What surprised him was the weight of the material.

'That's not my coat!' Steve exclaimed.

'But it is, Steve! It was in the back of your—'

'I don't care where it was! It's not my coat!'

Temple found it hard to understand why she was so vehement in repudiating this fashionable garment.

'Are you sure, dear?'

'I'm positive!' More quietly she asked: 'Is there anything in the pockets?'

He carefully checked both pockets. 'No, nothing.'

Steve pointed a finger towards the top of the coat. 'There should be a maker's name on the back of the collar somewhere.'

'Yes, I'm just looking for it.' Temple took the coat off the hanger and looked inside the collar. 'Ah, here we are!'

He turned the label towards the light to read the name. 'Margo . . .'

Superintendent Raine took his mackintosh off and handed it to Charlie, who hung it up in the little cloakroom. Through the closed door of the sitting-room he could hear someone playing the piano – one of Chopin's Nocturnes. Despite his air of businesslike efficiency Raine was a sensitive man and a lover of music. From the style of the playing he was able to recognise a woman's touch.

The music stopped when Charlie knocked on the door and went in to announce the visitor. A moment later Temple himself appeared.

'Hello, Superintendent!' he welcomed Raine warmly. 'Come along in!'

The Temples' coffee cups had been put back on the silver tray and a brandy glass was on the table beside Paul's chair. The book he had been reading had been placed on the arm, with the cover uppermost. It was the novel that had recently won the Booker McConnell prize.

Steve had come out from behind the baby grand piano.

'Good evening, Mrs Temple.' Raine gave her a courtly bow. 'You look better than you did a week ago.'

'Yes,' Steve smiled. 'I'm fine now, thank you very much.'

'I just happened to be passing and I thought I'd drop in and have a word with you.'

'Glad to see you.' Temple indicated a chair. 'Sit down. Can I get you a drink?'

'No, thank you. I'm afraid my day's work is not done yet.' Raine sat down, as usual leaning slightly forward. 'Well, we don't seem to have got very far during the past week. We've made enquiries about the coat, but we've drawn a blank. We've failed to find the owner, or even the shop where it was bought.'

'What about the makers?'

'We can't even locate the makers. According to all accounts, there isn't a coat firm called Margo – not in this country, at any rate.'

'I see.' Steve and Paul exchanged a glance. 'Did you check with the airport people?'

'Yes, and we've had no luck there either, I'm afraid. I suppose you haven't had any bright ideas, Mr Temple?'

'No, I'm afraid I haven't, except that . . . Well, I think the people who kidnapped Steve were labouring under the delusion that I was just about to investigate a case of some kind.'

'And you think the Mrs Temple incident was a warning to keep out?'

'Yes, I do.'

'Well, that's a possible explanation, I suppose,' Raine conceded dubiously. 'But what's the case?'

'You tell me.' Temple tapped his pipe out and reached for the tobacco jar. 'I never interfere in anything without an invitation. What's your biggest headache at the moment?'

'Oh, our biggest headache is The Fence – trying to find out who the devil he is. But we've had that headache for some time now. I doubt whether we'll ever solve it.'

Steve had gone back to the piano stool and was leafing through some sheet music, obviously intending not to intrude on the conversation; but she was drawn into it in spite of herself.

'What do you mean – The Fence?'

'Well, you know what a fence is, Mrs Temple?' Raine had to shift his position to face her.

'Yes – a man who receives stolen property.'

'That's right. Well, during the past twelve months there's been several robberies. I mean, really big stuff. The two jewellers in Leicester Square . . . the fur warehouse in Bond Street . . .'

'Lord Renton's place in Eaton Square,' Temple put in, as Raine hesitated.

'Yes, that's right. Well, it's our opinion that these particular jobs were all done . . .'

'. . . by the same gang!' Steve supplied, determined not to be outdone.

Raine laughed good-humouredly. 'No, Mrs Temple. Nothing quite as simple as that. We think – in fact, we know that the various jobs have been done by different people. We feel pretty confident, however, that the stolen property was, in every case, handled by the same person.'

'The Fence?'

'Yes, Mrs Temple. So far we've failed to find out who this fence is – or where he operates from. But sooner or later we've got to find him, because, at the moment, he's indirectly responsible for a great many of the robberies in this country.'

'Then I can see why you've got to find him,' Temple remarked drily.

'Still, we've no reason for thinking – no proof, as it were that Mrs Temple's experience had anything to do with The Fence.'

'No, Superintendent,' Temple said thoughtfully. 'No proof.'

There was a short silence, but Raine made no move to go. 'There *was* one thing I wanted to ask you. The day Mrs Temple disappeared you said something about a note – a telephone message – which was on the pad by the side of the bed.'

'Yes, of course!' Temple struck his brow with the flat of his hand. 'I forgot all about that! There was a note, Steve. It said: "Tell P. about L."'

'Oh, that was Laura Stafford,' Steve said dismissively. 'She telephoned one morning and said she wanted to see you. She seemed awfully disappointed when I said you were in New York.'

'Who's Laura Stafford?' Temple enquired.

'She's a journalist – or rather she was several years ago.' Steve forsook the piano stool and moved over to the sofa. 'We used to see quite a bit of each other when I worked in Fleet Street. Then she left and married a man called Kelburn.'

'Kelburn?' Temple echoed, with surprise. 'George Kelburn?'

'Yes, I think so.'

'Very wealthy. North country. She's his second wife.'

'That's right.' Steve leaned back and crossed her legs. Raine bent his head and dutifully studied his fingernails. 'Anyway, when I said you were in New York she said she'd get in touch with you later. I thought nothing of it at the time, but a couple of days later I bumped into Laura in Freeman and Bentley's and naturally, I mentioned the telephone call, and to my amazement she said she hadn't 'phoned.'

Raine looked up sharply. 'She said she hadn't?'

'That's right, Superintendent. She said she certainly had no wish to consult Paul about anything.' Steve turned to Temple, whose expression showed his scepticism. 'Darling, why were you surprised when I mentioned the name Kelburn?'

'Well, coming over on the 'plane a man called Langdon introduced himself to me. He works for George Kelburn. Apparently Kelburn's having trouble with his daughter and he's asked Langdon to try and sort it out.'

27

'Yes, I've heard of Miss Kelburn,' Raine said meaningfully. 'Julia, by name.'

'That's right.'

'Always in the newspapers. She must be quite a handful, that young lady. I don't envy Mr Langdon his assignment.' He put his hands on his knees to push himself upright. 'Well, I'll be making a move. Glad you're feeling better, Mrs Temple.'

Raine had been gone for an hour and Steve had announced her intention of going to bed early when the doorbell rang and they heard Charlie going to answer it. A few moments later his head came round the door.

'What is it, Charlie?'

'Are you in or out, Mr Temple?'

'At a quick glance, I should say we're in.'

'Well, there's a Mr Langdon would like to see you. Looks like a Yank to me.'

'Yes – he is a Yank, as you so elegantly put it, Charlie. Show the gentleman in.'

'Yes, sir.'

'Langdon?' Steve asked. 'Is this the man you met on the 'plane?'

'Yes.'

'Did you ask him to call?'

'Not in so many words, but I said if I could be of use any time I'd be pleased to see him.'

Like Raine, Langdon refused the offer of a drink, but accepted a chair. Steve resigned herself to being a listener to another of Temple's interviews. She always admired his capacity for making people feel that a visit from them was just what he had been hoping for and that he had all the time in the world to listen to their confidences.

'I've already had more than my share of drink this evening,' Langdon said with a sigh. 'Which isn't surprising – considering.'

'Why, is the Kelburn business getting you down?'

'It certainly is.'

'You've seen Julia, I take it?'

'Yes, half a dozen times. It's hopeless – she has every intention of doing precisely what she wants.'

'And what about the young man she's keen on – Tony Wyman?'

'I went to see Wyman last night.' An expression of distaste crossed Langdon's face. 'At The Hide and Seek. He completely denied that he and Julia were engaged. He just laughed when I said that Kelburn would pay him twenty-five grand not to see her again. He became quite offensive. Said he wouldn't marry the girl if she was the last piece on earth. So far as he was concerned Kelburn could keep his twenty-five grand and his daughter too!' Langdon sighed again.

'What a charming young man!'

'You can say that again, Mrs Temple. I wasn't exactly enthralled by Master Wyman!'

'Do you think he was telling the truth?'

'I don't know, Temple. He sounded convincing and yet it just doesn't add up. Everyone I've spoken to swears he's got his eye on her. Temple, I know this is a bit of a cheek, but do you think you could make one or two enquiries for me?'

Steve shot Temple a warning look, but he seemed to be more interested in refilling his pipe.

'All right, Langdon, we'll get on the grapevine and see what we can do.'

'That's mighty kind of you,' Langdon said effusively. 'I appreciate it, I really do.'

'Then how about changing your mind and having a drink?'

As Steve turned away to hide her exasperation at Temple's excessive hospitality, Langdon put his head on one side. 'There's nothing I'd like better.'

Temple raised his head from the pillow at the third ring of the telephone, but no sooner was he properly awake than it stopped.

'Probably realised they were dialling the wrong number,' Steve said beside him. He could tell from her voice that she had been lying awake.

'What time is it?'

'Struck three a few minutes ago.'

'Couldn't you get to sleep?'

'I keep thinking of Laura Kelburn. It must be awful having a daughter like Julia. Paul, do you think she was lying when she said she hadn't telephoned me?'

'I can't see why she—' Paul stopped as the 'phone started ringing again.' Who could be telephoning us at this hour?'

'Take your time, Paul. If they really want us they won't ring off.'

Temple waited for a little while before switching the light on and picking up the 'phone.

'Hello.'

'Is that Paul Temple?' A woman's voice, speaking softly, as if she was afraid of being overheard.

'Yes, speaking.'

'This is Mrs Kelburn . . .' There was a crackling on the line and he could hardly catch the name.

'Who?'

'Mrs Kelburn . . . Laura Kelburn . . .'

'Oh, good evening – er – good morning, Mrs Kelburn.'

'Mr Temple, I'm sorry to disturb you at this time of night, but – I've got to see you.' There was desperation in her voice as she added: 'It really is important.'

'Well – what is it you want to see me about?'

'About – about Julia. My stepdaughter.'

'What about Julia?' Temple asked, not trying very hard to conceal his impatience.

'When can I see you, Mr Temple?' She was still speaking so softly that he could hardly hear her. 'Will nine o'clock be all right? I've got your address so . . .'

'Look, Mrs Kelburn, I'm quite prepared to see you, but first of all I must know what this is all about.'

'I've told you. It's about my stepdaughter – Julia.'

'Yes, I know, but what about Julia?'

There was a long pause, but no indication that she had rung off. Temple wondered whether someone had taken the receiver from her. Then suddenly she said very quickly but quite distinctly: 'She's going to be murdered.'

There came a click and Temple was left listening to the dialling tone.

'Hello, Steve!' Temple had finished his toast and marmalade and was pouring himself a second cup of coffee before his wife appeared for breakfast the next morning. 'You're nice and late this morning!'

'Yes, I know,' Steve admitted wryly. 'I didn't get to sleep until five o'clock.'

'It's not surprising. We didn't stop talking until half past four. I'll pour you some coffee.'

'No, I don't want any coffee, dear. I'll just have the orange juice. What time is it, anyway?'

'Twenty past nine.'

'My word, we are late . . .'

'Yes – and so's your friend, Laura Kelburn. She said she'd be here by . . . 'He was stopped by a long peal on the door-bell. 'This will be her now.'

'Do you want me to stay?'

'Yes, of course.'

Temple had time to pour an orange juice and put it down at Steve's side of the table before Charlie opened the door.

'Superintendent Raine would like to—' Charlie broke off scandalised as the Superintendent pushed in past him. He had not even taken time to remove his overcoat.

'Excuse me! Mr Temple, may I have a word with you?'

'Yes, of course. All right, Charlie.' Temple dismissed Charlie with a reassuring nod. 'What is it, Raine? What's happened?'

'We picked a girl out of the river – about two hours ago. She'd been strangled. It was George Kelburn's daughter.'

'Julia Kelburn?'

'Yes. But that isn't everything.' Raine paused for a moment. 'The dead girl was wearing a coat. There was a name label stitched inside the collar. We've seen that name before, sir.'

Temple nodded. He was already ahead of Raine.

'Margo?'

CHAPTER II

Dead Lucky

'Well, there's one person who won't be surprised by the murder, Superintendent. That's Julia's stepmother – Laura Kelburn.'

Raine had accepted coffee and Charlie had deigned to bring an extra cup. The three were sitting round the breakfast table.

'Why do you say that, Mrs Temple?'

It was Temple who answered. 'Mrs Kelburn telephoned – at three o'clock this morning, mark you – and made an appointment to see me at nine o'clock. When I asked her why she wanted to see me she said it was about Julia – and that her stepdaughter was going to be murdered.'

'This is extraordinary!' Raine shook his head in bewilderment. 'Quite extraordinary!'

'I agree. When I picked up the 'phone and . . .'

'No, you don't understand,' Raine cut in. 'I've seen Mrs Kelburn – about an hour ago. I went to the house in the Boltons. She didn't say anything about telephoning you – on the contrary she seemed staggered by the news of the murder. If anything, I think she was even more shaken by the news than her husband.'

'She never mentioned the 'phone call?'

'Not a word.'

'How did Mr Kelburn react?' Steve asked.

'He was pretty badly shaken, of course, but I had the impression he'd been worried about his daughter for some time. She mixed with a pretty notorious crowd, you know, Mrs Temple.'

'Yes. She was friendly with a man called Tony Wyman.'

'I'm checking on Mr Wyman. I've got an appointment to see . . .' Raine broke off. A receiver had been plugged in to the telephone socket in the dining-room and its bell had started to ring.

'Excuse me.' Temple swivelled round in his chair and reached for the instrument.

'Paul Temple?'

'Yes, speaking.'

'This is Mike Langdon, Temple . . .'

'Yes. I recognised your voice. Good morning, Langdon.'

'Temple, I've got some terrible news . . .'

'We've heard about Julia Kelburn.' Temple cut the agitated recital short. 'The Superintendent's with me now.'

'Then I expect he's told you all the details?'

'Well, yes. It's a pretty awful business.' Then, more sympathetically: 'It must have been a shock for you, Langdon.'

'Yes, it was – a terrible shock. I never realised the poor kid was so mixed up . . . But look, Temple – I want to ask you a favour.' Paul met Steve's eyes. Langdon's voice was audible throughout the room. 'Kelburn's determined that the person responsible for this shan't escape. He's anxious to make the fullest possible investigation – expense no object.'

'Well?' Temple prompted non-committally.

'He'd like to see you, Temple. He'd like you to call round this morning, if possible. They live in the Boltons, the house is called "Northdown".'

'I see.' Temple raised his eyebrows enquiringly at Steve, who nodded. 'Does that go for Mrs Kelburn, too?'

'What do you mean?'

'Does Mrs Kelburn want me to call round?'

'Why, yes, of course.' Langdon was puzzled by the question. 'I imagine so. She hasn't said otherwise.'

Temple calculated for a moment, then said: 'Tell Mr Kelburn I'll be there at twelve o'clock.'

'Right! Thanks a lot. I appreciate it . . .'

Temple put the receiver down, cutting off Langdon's protestations of gratitude.

'Excuse my asking, Mr Temple,' Raine said, 'but who's this fellow Langdon?'

'He's one of Kelburn's right-hand men. I met him on the 'plane coming over from New York. Kelburn sent for him. He apparently thought Langdon might be able to reform his daughter. I understand he'd got her out of one or two little scrapes in New York.'

'All the way from New York because Kelburn couldn't cope with his own daughter?' Raine grinned at Steve. 'Sounds a bit far-fetched.'

'I don't know,' Temple said. 'We never knew Julia Kelburn. We don't even know what her father was up against. However, Langdon's main job was to try and buy off Tony Wyman.'

'That's interesting. What happened?'

'Wyman told Langdon he couldn't care less about Julia – in no uncertain terms.'

'Mm.' Raine had brought a notebook out of his pocket and opened it at a page where there was a marker. He tapped his teeth with a pencil. 'This chap Langdon – is he about forty, dark wavy hair, medium height, uses a pretty exotic aftershave?'

Temple smiled. 'Yes, that's him!'

'He was hovering about when I interviewed Kelburn and his wife, but they didn't introduce me. They were pretty upset, of course.'

Leaning over so that she could take a peek at Raine's notebook, Steve was surprised to see that the page was covered with as many doodles and drawings as words. The Superintendent drew a circle round one of his sketches.

'Would you say there's been anything between Langdon and Julia Kelburn?'

'I don't think so, but I wouldn't know, of course. You'd better ask Langdon that question.'

'I will,' Raine promised, putting away his notebook and standing up. 'Thank you for the coffee, Mrs Temple.'

'Our pleasure, Superintendent.'

'You've no objection, I take it,' Temple asked casually, as he ushered Raine to the door, 'if I go along and see Kelburn?'

'Not the slightest, Mr Temple.' Raine gave him a smile and a long, straight look. 'Not the slightest. It's a free country so they tell me . . .'

'It isn't that I mistrust the police, Mr Temple. I just think that a case of this kind demands a more imaginative approach than the average police officer is capable of.'

The emotional stress he was under had made George Kelburn's Yorkshire accent more pronounced. He was a burly man with the paunch and podgy cheeks of someone who can afford more whisky than was good for him, and it was evident that he had been seeking solace from the decanter. He was wearing a black tie with the dark blue suit which a skilful tailor had constructed to mask his bulk.

'Mr Kelburn, I've worked with the police now for many years and I can assure you that the men at Scotland Yard are shrewd, intelligent and highly efficient.'

Since greeting Temple, Kelburn had not invited him to sit down. The furniture of the room was luxurious but brash and showy. Standing on the brilliantly patterned carpet Temple could look down through the window at a tiny walled garden.

'Efficient, yes, maybe. But slow – slow. That's the trouble – damned slow. My daughter's been murdered, Mr Temple my only child . . .' The tears were springing again to Kelburn's eyes. 'I'll give anything to find the swine responsible for that murder. Just name the fee . . .'

Kelburn was chairman of over fifteen companies and believed that he could buy anyone's services with a snap of his fingers and a flourish of his cheque book.

'You don't solve a case of this kind simply by paying someone a fat fee, Mr Kelburn,' Temple said quietly. 'The whole problem is far too—'

He saw Kelburn's moist eyes focus over his left shoulder and turned round. A woman who looked about fifteen years younger than Kelburn had come quietly into the room.

'Oh, there you are, Laura! I was wondering where you'd got to. Mr Temple – may I introduce my wife?'

'How do you do, Mrs Kelburn? I believe you know Steve . . .' As they shook hands Temple felt the chunky rings on her fingers. She had put on a dark grey suit, but her nails were painted and her auburn hair was as crisp as if she had just come from the hairdressers.

'I do indeed. Is she well?'

'Thank you, yes. She was looking forward to seeing you this morning.'

'This morning?' Laura echoed, obviously puzzled.

'Yes. We were expecting you to call at nine o'clock as arranged, but obviously this business . . .'

'I'm sorry, Mr Temple, but I don't understand.'

'Were you under the impression that my wife was coming to see you?' Kelburn demanded.

'I was indeed.'

'What made you think she wanted to see you?' Langdon's nasal drawl gave the question an unflattering implication.

'The fact that she telephoned me in the early hours of this morning and said that she wanted to.'

Laura Kelburn stepped back, staring at Temple in amazement. 'I – I telephoned you?'

'Yes. About three o'clock a.m.'

'But that's nonsense!' she exclaimed, throwing an appealing glance at her husband.

Kelburn crossed to his wife and put a hand under her elbow. 'I can assure you my wife didn't 'phone you, Mr Temple. We occupy the same bedroom. If she'd made a telephone call at that hour of the morning I'd certainly have known about it.'

She said: 'What exactly am I supposed to have 'phoned you about?'

'You told me that you suspected . . .' Temple hesitated.

'Suspected what?' she prompted him rapidly.

'That your stepdaughter was going to be murdered.'

Laura's eyes widened and her hand covered her mouth.

'Good God!' Kelburn stared accusingly at Temple, as if he was responsible for everything that had happened. 'But this is ridiculous!'

'Are you serious, Temple?' Langdon asked angrily.

'Wait a minute!' Laura had recovered her poise quickly.

'This is the second time I'm supposed to have made a mysterious telephone call.' She turned to Temple. 'I met your wife a couple of weeks ago and she had some strange story about having spoken to me on the 'phone – and my saying I wanted to see you.'

'And you didn't want to see me?'

'Of course not!' Laura dismissed the idea emphatically. 'I didn't even 'phone . . .'

'Someone did,' Temple said quietly, then abruptly changed the subject. 'Mrs Kelburn, your husband has asked me to investigate this affair and I think perhaps you might be able to help me.'

'How, exactly?' she asked, a shade brittle.

'Well, you can start by telling me where Julia bought her clothes from.'

'I'm afraid I don't know where she bought her clothes from. She wasn't very fussy about her dress, you know.' From Laura's tone it was clear that Julia Kelburn had been more than a handful.

'Could you find out?'

Laura shrugged. 'Yes, I suppose so.'

'I'm interested in the coat she was wearing at the time of the murder,' Temple persisted. 'There was a label inside with the name "Margo" on it.'

'Margo?'

'Yes. Does that name mean anything to you?'

'No, I'm afraid it doesn't. But I'll make enquiries if you like?'

'I'd be grateful if you would, Mrs Kelburn.'

Kelburn had been listening to the exchange with increasing impatience. 'Mr Temple, surely there's something we can do – something just a little more progressive than enquiring about a coat?'

'Take it easy, George,' Langdon drawled. 'Mr Temple knows what he's doing.'

Temple looked pointedly at his watch, glad of his cue to escape from an atmosphere that had become faintly hostile.

'You have my 'phone number, Mrs Kelburn, if you want to get in touch with me?'

'Yes, of course . . .' she said absent-mindedly, then quickly corrected herself. 'No, I'm afraid I haven't.'

'It's in the book,' Temple said with a smile. 'Now, if you'll excuse me, Mr Kelburn, I have a lunch appointment.'

In fact, Temple's lunch appointment was with Steve at a small restaurant just off the Bayswater Road where they were well known. It was while they were having coffee that she came out with what had been on her mind all through the meal.

'Paul, do you think the people who kidnapped me were responsible for the murder?'

'Yes, I do. And I think I know why they kidnapped you, Steve.' Temple leaned forward and lowered his voice. 'While I was in America a report appeared in one of the Continental newspapers . . . Well, I've got it in my pocket.' He took out his wallet, extracted a folded newspaper cutting and handed it across the table. 'Read it for yourself.'

She unfolded the paper and smoothed it flat on the tablecloth. The report was quite brief. After a few lines about the multiple activities of the master criminal known as The Fence, it stated that the celebrated criminologist, Paul Temple, had cut short his American tour at the request of Scotland Yard and was returning post-haste to London.

'The Fence is that man Raine mentioned?'

'Yes.'

'Is it true that Scotland Yard have asked you to help them?'

'No, darling – it's just a newspaper story. Sir Graham and I have never even discussed The Fence.'

'But you think that someone read this and . . .'

'I think The Fence himself read it and believed it. Remember what that man said to you, Steve. "We did it as a warning and to prove that it was possible, Mrs Temple."'

Steve nodded, thoughtful and serious.

'From now on you've got to watch your step, dear. Get Charlie to answer the door. Don't go anywhere on your own if you can help it. Always leave a message as to your whereabouts. Don't act on any telephone calls without checking. Well – you know the routine.'

'Yes,' she said with resignation, 'I know the routine.'

Temple had been given a lift back from the Boltons by Mike Langdon, but Steve had driven to the restaurant in her MG Metro, and had been lucky enough to find a parking meter close by. Traffic on the Bayswater Road was thick and a hundred yards from Marble Arch it had slowed to a sluggish crawl.

'Relax, darling,' Steve said, with a smile. 'I don't mind this, I'm used to it.'

'Delighted to hear it. And you can relax too, your hair's fine.'

'My hair?'

'Isn't that why you keep looking in the mirror?'

'As a matter of fact I was watching the car behind. The Escort driven by a man in dark glasses. It was parked outside the flat when I left and it was behind me when I drove to the restaurant.'

Temple did not turn round. As the traffic began to move he said quickly: 'Take this turning on the left. Yes, this one!'

Steve obeyed instinctively and the car lurched as she made the turn. Temple lowered the anti-dazzle flap and used the vanity mirror to check on the cars behind.

'Yes, he's following us all right. Steve, pull in to the kerb behind that taxi that's stopping.'

'What's the idea?'

'I'm getting out. I want you to drive straight home. I'll see you there.'

Steve knew better than to question Temple when he was in this mood. He had the door open before she stopped. The driver of the Escort had two options. Either he could pass the Metro and risk losing it or pull in and take the chance of being spotted. Inexperienced at car tailing, he was braking hesitantly when Temple ran out from the kerb, opened the door on the passenger side and slid into the seat.

'Here, what's the big idea,' the man in dark glasses protested, 'getting into my car like this?'

'Keep going!' Temple told him crisply. 'I'll explain later.'

'Who the hell are you?'

Steve had already accelerated away and drivers behind had started a cadenza on their horns.

'Drive on. People are getting impatient.'

'I don't give a damn what people . . .'

'Drive on! And there's no need to follow that Metro, I can tell you all you want to know about it.'

As the engine almost stalled the other man rammed the lever with a crunch into a lower gear. 'What the hell are you talking about?'

'I think you know what I'm talking about. You've been following that car all the way from Eaton Square. Now I suggest you drive into the Park – we can have a little talk there.'

'I—' He started to protest again, then suddenly caved in. 'Yes, all right.'

'I should switch the engine off, Mr Wyman.'

Docile now, Tony Wyman reached forward and turned the key. Following Temple's instructions he had driven into Hyde

Park and stopped on a yellow line on the stretch parallel to Bayswater Road.

'You recognised me, then?'

'Yes, I recognised you.' Temple smiled. It would have taken more than a pair of dark glasses to disguise the pop singer, with his outrageous hairstyle. 'Now, what can I do for you? Why are you following us around?'

'I've read a lot about you in the papers, Mr Temple, and I thought – well, I'm in dead trouble, see? And I thought maybe you could sort of give me a line. I hung around your flat hoping to catch you, but I couldn't pluck up enough courage to . . .'

'All right, so you have a problem?' Temple was watching a yellow delivery van with a rent-a-van sign painted on the side, which had cruised past slowly and stopped a couple of hundred yards further down.

'It's the police, Mr Temple. They've put the wind up me. That Superintendent Raine gave me a proper going over. Practically accused me of doin' the murder.'

'You mean Julia Kelburn?'

'Yes, and I never even knew she'd been killed, straight I didn't. That chap Raine was at me for the best part of an hour, but all I could tell him was that I finished at the club just after one and went straight home.'

'Just how friendly were you with Julia Kelburn?'

'Depends what you mean by friendly.'

'How did you meet her?'

'Some of the gang – the reg'lars – brought her to the club one night. She was dressed all sloppy like with her hair all combed up and dyed. I thought at first she was one of them punks. But we got talkin' a bit and she seemed to go for me. Next time she come in, I hardly knew her. She looked like a film star.'

'Did you know her father was well off?'

Down the road the yellow van was taking advantage of a lull in the traffic to make a three-point turn.

'Well, not at first – she never let on. But later she started throwing the lolly around and I guessed somebody had the dough. She wasn't a bad kid. I was fond of her in a funny sort of way, but – well, she started getting in my hair. Hanging around the club, meeting me in restaurants, waiting for me at the TV studios – you know how it is.'

'No, I don't know how it is. You tell me.'

'Well, you know – she was a bit of a mixed-up kid. Bit dotty, perhaps, I don't know. Spent quids with one of those psychiwhatsits.'

Gathering speed, the yellow van was now heading back towards the parked Escort.

'Oh – who told you that?'

'She did. She used to visit a shrink in Wimpole Street. Benkaray, I think the name was. Yes, that's right – Dr Benkaray.'

'Did you tell the Superintendent about this?'

'No, I didn't tell him any more than was necessary.'

Keeping an eye on the yellow van, Temple had a hand on the door lever.

'I know the police only too well. When I was a kid in Bermondsey I –' Wyman broke off and his voice rose to a falsetto shriek. 'Hi, look at this van!' The truck had suddenly veered left, just as if a steering linkage had broken, but instead of braking the driver was accelerating. 'He's coming straight for us!'

Temple flung his door open and yelled: 'Get out, quick!'

He dived out through the door, hitting the grass with his shoulder and rolling over. As he went he heard Wyman cursing his sticking door. There came the sickening thud of metal on metal, the tinkling of glass, a hiss of steam, followed by a high-pitched scream of agony.

A passing taxi driver had seen the accident and had the good sense to drive straight to the nearest call-box and dial 999. A police car, ambulance and fire brigade van were there within minutes. While the ambulance men slid the truck driver into their vehicle and the firemen cut Wyman free of the tangled wreckage of the car, Temple gave the police a preliminary report of the incident.

'We'll want you to give us a written statement, sir,' the patrolman said.

'Yes, I know. But in the meantime I suggest you call Superintendent Raine at Scotland Yard. Tell him someone just damn nearly killed Tony Wyman and Paul Temple.'

Raine was at Paddington Hospital within ten minutes of Temple arriving there in the police car. Despite the fuss he had made, Tony Wyman was not seriously injured. He had escaped with a couple of broken fingers, some nasty cuts and a mass of bruises. According to the doctor who had attended him he would not be detained in hospital.

'That must have been quite a spectacular little crash,' Raine said.

'It was – and a deliberate one too.'

'A good thing you managed to get clear.'

'I was dead lucky. What have they done with that truck driver?'

'He's at Paddington Green police station. Got away with a few bruises and a cut cheek. He was carrying his licence so we know who he is. A Scot, name of Ted Angus.'

'Ted Angus?'

'Do you know him?'

'I don't think so.'

'I've been on to Glasgow. They know him but have never been able to pin anything on him. He's done all sorts of jobs. Barker in a fairground, Wall of Death rider. May have been mixed up in a couple of smash-and-grab jobs but always got clear. You know, I hardly think it was you he was after. It was Wyman's car.'

'Maybe you're right. Are you going to charge him?'

'We can only hold him for an hour or two but I intend to try and make him talk. You can come along if you feel up to it.'

'Oh, I'm up to it. Just give me a moment to 'phone my wife.'

But even Raine's and Temple's questioning failed to extract any admission from the tough little Scot. His story was that the steering had broken and he was sticking to that, knowing full well the whole front of the truck was smashed.

'What do you make of him?' Temple asked, as the cell door was closed on Angus. He was still protesting vociferously at being 'treated like a criminal'.

'About as straight as the Tower of Pisa, but we're still going to have to let him go.'

The Temples were just finishing tea when Charlie came in to announce that a Mrs Kelburn had called.

'Show her in, Charlie. And take this tray away.'

'Are you expecting Laura?' Steve asked.

'No, but I did ask her to find out where Julia bought her clothes.'

Laura Kelburn was still wearing the same dark suit, but she had added a pair of ear-rings and a gold neck-chain.

'No, I won't, thank you, Mr Temple,' she said, in reply to the offer of a drink. 'I'm in rather a hurry. I'm dining with some people in Hampstead. Mr Temple, I've made one or two enquiries about Julia's clothes, and I've been through her wardrobe. There's nothing with the name Margo on it, but I've discovered that most of her clothes – most of the respectable clothes, at any rate – were bought from a shop in Ogden Street called Daphne Drake Limited. You must have heard of it, Steve.'

'Yes, I've heard of it. It's a very good shop.'

'Did Julia have many clothes?' Temple asked.

'Yes, she did, but she was a frightfully erratic sort of person. She'd probably wear nothing but jeans and a sweater for a month or so, and then suddenly buy herself half a dozen dresses and suits. There was no telling what she'd do. Unfortunately, it wasn't only her clothes that she was erratic about.'

'What do you mean?'

Laura Kelburn's mouth twisted with distaste. 'Well – she wasn't exactly careful about her choice of friends, was she? Of course, the trouble was George wouldn't take her in hand. He wouldn't hear a word against her. Understandable, I suppose, but rather irritating at times.'

'Did you try to take her in hand, Mrs Kelburn?'

'No,' she said, affronted by the question. 'It wasn't my job.'

'But you were quite good friends?'

Laura pondered that for a moment. 'Yes – we were, considering. But, the trouble really started when George got a bee in his bonnet about this Tony Wyman person and tried to lay the law down. It was too late – you just couldn't do that sort of thing with Julia. Tell her she couldn't have something, and she'd immediately want it.'

'How is your husband, Laura?' Steve enquired.

'He's still very upset, of course – it's been a terrible shock for him, but the doctor's given him some dope. He was lying down when I left. I suppose there's no news, Mr Temple? The police have no idea who did it?'

'No. At least, I certainly haven't heard anything, Mrs Kelburn.'

Laura picked her crocodile handbag off the floor and stood up. 'Well, I must be going.'

'I'm very grateful to you for calling. You'll let me know if you come across anything you think might be of any importance?'

'Yes, of course. I certainly will, Mr Temple.'

'I hope she enjoys her dinner,' Temple remarked, when Steve came back from showing the visitor out.

'You don't like her, do you, Paul?'

'No – but I'm glad she called. I wonder if this Daphne Drake place is worth investigating.'

'Well, I can tell you one thing, the coat that was left in my car at the airport wasn't bought from Daphne Drake's.'

'How do you know?'

'The weight of the material. And it wasn't their style. They have much more expensive stuff than that. They have some really lovely things.' Steve put her head on one side and gave Paul a look. 'You know, I think I ought to go along there tomorrow morning, and make a few enquiries.'

'I know the sort of enquiries you'd make!' Temple laughed. 'Still, it's not a bad idea.'

'Thank you, darling.'

'But, Steve—'

'Yes, dear?'

'One dress – one only, remember . . .'

Dr M. C. Benkaray was in the telephone book with an address in Wimpole Street.

'I hope he doesn't shut up shop at five o'clock.'

Steve broke off playing the piano while Temple dialled the number. 'Why are you so anxious to talk to this Dr Benkaray, Paul?'

'Tony Wyman told me that Julia Kelburn recently consulted a psychiatrist. I thought it might be a good idea to find out what her trouble was—' Temple broke off and took his hand away from the mouthpiece as the ringing tone stopped.

'Dr Benkaray's practice.'

Temple hesitated, puzzled by the man's accent. 'May I speak to the doctor, please?'

'What's your name?'

'Temple. Paul Temple.'

'Just hold on a minute, please.'

Watching him, Steve saw two lines appear between his brow, always a sign that he was adding two and two and making five. 'What is it, Paul?'

'I could swear that the man on the other end – Hello! Is that Dr Benkaray?'

'No, this is Dr Benkaray's secretary.' The voice was masculine but more like that of a car salesman than a doctor's secretary. 'The doctor is out of town.'

'My name is Temple. I'd like to make an appointment—'

'Then I suggest you 'phone again towards the end of the month.'

'But surely—'

'Any time after the twenty-fifth. I shall be pleased to make an appointment for you then.'

'But I'm afraid that's too—'

'Goodbye, Mr Temple.'

Slowly Temple put the receiver down.

'Well, I'm damned! He cut me short and rang off. By Timothy, if that's the secretary I wonder what the doctor's like.'

'Did you think you recognised the person who answered first?'

Temple nodded. 'He sounded exactly like that truck driver who nearly wrote me off. Ted Angus.'

Steve was only forty minutes late for her rendezvous with Temple. They had arranged to meet in the cocktail bar of a small club near Ebury Street.

'Hello, Steve! I thought you were never coming! Did you buy up the whole shop?'

'No, darling, I didn't.'

She sat down on the button-leather bench beside him. One of the club waiters, in a short green jacket, came over to the table.

'Can I get you anything, madam?'

'I'd like a dry sherry.'

Temple pointed to his own glass. 'I'll have the same again.'

'Yes, sir. A Tio Pepe and a dry martini.'

'Well, Steve?' Temple knew from the way she kept glancing at him with a faint smile on her lips that she'd had a successful morning. He hoped the bill would not be too high.

'I've got some news for you, Mr Temple!'

'About Margo?'

'No, they've never heard of the name – at least, they said they haven't. But I'll tell you who they have heard of, Paul. Dr Benkaray.'

'Dr Benkaray?'

'Yes, she's a customer of theirs.'

'*She's* a – are you serious, Steve?'

'I'm quite serious, darling.'

'I took it for granted Benkaray was a man, I never thought – By Timothy, I must watch my step. I'm slipping, Steve! Go on, tell me what happened.'

'Dr Benkaray bought a coat from Daphne Drake's and they were asked to post it to her – she's living in the country somewhere.'

'Where, do you know?'

'At a place called Westerton. I don't know the address. Where is Westerton – the name seemed familiar?'

'It's in Kent, about forty miles from here. Rather a nice little place. There's a very good pub there called The Red Hart. We stayed at it one weekend, about six or seven years ago.'

'Oh, I remember The Red Hart. The landlord was a wizened little man with a bald head. It's rather an odd place for a psychiatrist to live, isn't it? I should have thought she'd have lived in town.'

'She has a place in town, in Wimpole Street.'

'Oh, yes, of course.'

'Your sherry, madam.' The waiter had arrived with their drinks. 'And a dry martini for you, sir.'

Temple paid the waiter and raised his glass to his wife.

'Steve, I'm very interested in this Dr Benkaray, for several reasons. One: Julia Kelburn consulted her, and two: I still think it was that chap Angus who answered the telephone.'

'Which means, I suppose, we're going to spend the weekend at Westerton?'

'Yes, darling.'

It was hard to believe that such a remote and unspoilt village as Westerton was less than fifty miles from London. It was in the middle of a hop-growing area and the characteristic cones of the oast-houses jutted up from the farms in the countryside around. The Red Hart was a traditional pub which had changed little since the Temples had stayed there seven years earlier. Their visit must have been quite an event in the village, for Fred Harcourt recognised them immediately and gave them a warm welcome. He showed them up to his best double bedroom, the same one they'd occupied on the previous occasion. Temple took care to stoop as he crossed the raised lintel. He had painful memories of bumping his head on the beams of the low roof.

In the bar down below some of the evening regulars had already come in. Temple exchanged nods and smiles with a couple of rustic characters who appeared to recognise him. They made way respectfully for Steve when they saw she intended to sit on a bar stool and kept glancing at her with covert admiration.

'Still brewing your own beer, Mr Harcourt?'

'Oh, yes, Mr Temple. We get people from miles away, even London, just to see what real beer tastes like.'

'Draw us two pints, please.'

Fred fetched a couple of tankards and began to pull on his decorated levers. The passing years had shrunk him, his features were more wizened and his head balder, but he still had the same bright, humorous eyes.

'There you are, sir. Two nice foaming tankards.'

'Paul, am I supposed to—'

'Talking of people from London,' Temple said, pretending not to hear Steve's protest. 'Have you come across a Dr Benkaray in these parts?'

'You mean the lady doctor – who took Miller's croft in Vine Lane?'

'Yes, I should imagine that's the same person.'

'She doesn't practise down here, does she?' Steve asked, brushing a wisp of foam from her upper lip.

'No, Mrs Temple – at least, not with the locals. She's a specialist. Nervous diseases, I think – or something like that. Got a very nice place, they tell me, two cottages knocked into one. Everybody says how nice it is. Mrs Fletcher, one of my regulars, used to be the daily. Lovely place, she says it is.'

'You haven't met the doctor?' Temple asked.

'No. Just seen her around in the village.' Fred was wiping the counter with a cloth. He added ambiguously: 'Striking-looking woman.'

'Has she many friends – locally, I mean?'

'No, I reckon Mrs Fletcher knows her as well as most – although she doesn't work for her now. Hasn't been up there for almost a year. Always speaks well of the doctor, though, does Mrs Fletcher. Says she's a real lady.'

'Where is Vine Lane?' Steve had taken a good pull of her ale and appeared to be enjoying it.

'It's about four miles from here. The cottages stand on their own. Wouldn't be another house for about quarter of a mile. But it's very pretty. There's a nice little wood and a stream running right across the end of the lane.'

'Mr Harcourt!' The chubby girl who was helping behind the bar had received an order for a Campari and found that the bottle standing upside down on its dispenser was empty.

'Coming, Maisie!' said Fred, feeling for his keys. 'Excuse me, Mr Temple.'

'Yes, of course.'

'Oh.' Fred paused. 'I meant to ask you. Would you like John to put your car away, sir? We've got a private lock-up if you'd like one.'

'No thanks, Mr Harcourt, we shall probably go for a drive later on.'

'Are you going to see this Mrs Fletcher?' Steve asked, as the landlord bustled away.

'I might do later, darling, but it's a bit tricky. I don't want to attract too much attention. What do you think of this beer?'

Steve chuckled and peered into her tankard, which was still three-quarters full. 'If I finish this I'll certainly attract attention – I'll be sparked out!'

They had driven down from London in Temple's car, the 3500 Rover Vanden Plas EFI. It gave him the performance of a BMW and the comfort of a Rolls without being too ostentatious. Steve was humming happily as the village fell behind them and the countryside, still luminous in the afterglow of the sun, spread out on either side of them. As far as they could see there were ranks upon ranks of hops in the early stages of growth. A Land Rover coming in the opposite direction had already switched its lights on and as he passed Temple did the same.

About three miles from the village they came to a narrow lane which emerged from a wood to meet the read just short of a sharp bend. A telephone call-box stood at the junction beside a signpost.

'Can you read what it says, Steve?'

'Put your headlights up.'

Temple switched to main beam.

'Vine—' Steve was leaning forward trying to decipher the sign. 'Vine Lane. This is it.'

'Right. We'll park here.' Temple pulled the car on to the grass verge where obviously other drivers had stopped to use the call-box. 'Do you feel like a little stroll?'

'Isn't it rather dark?'

'Not really. Your eyes will soon adjust. Anyway, I've got a torch.'

'I wish I hadn't tried to finish that beer,' Steve said, gingerly putting a foot to the ground.

Vine Lane was a narrow track with occasional passing places. There was a line of grass growing in the middle but the marks of wheels showed that vehicles had recently been up and down. A hundred yards from the road the trees had thickened enough to meet over their heads and all at once it seemed very much darker.

'Dr Benkaray has certainly chosen a lonely spot. Still no sign of any cottage.'

'How much further do you want to go, Paul? If I'd known we were out for a hike I'd have put on walking shoes.'

'We'll go as far as that bend ahead.'

The normal friendly chatter of birds had died down with the coming of darkness; the only sound of life was the persistent hooting of an owl somewhere in the wood, and the grunting of some night creature on the prowl. At the bend Temple stopped and scrambled up the bank for a better view.

'Can you see anything, Paul?'

'Yes, I can see a light. About a quarter of a mile, I'd guess.'

'Do you think it's the cott—'

'Sh, Steve! Quiet a minute.'

'Can you hear—'

'SH!'

Straining her ears Steve realised that the sound of the animal grunting had changed in quality. Now it was more like – someone in pain calling for help!

'Paul—!'

But Temple was already slithering down the bank. 'There's someone in the wood, badly hurt.'

Using the torch now, he found a gap in the hedge and with Steve on his heels began to push in through the undergrowth. 'Where are you?' he shouted.

'Here,' a weak voice gasped. 'Over – here.'

'Hold my hand, Steve,' Temple said, turning half left and playing the torch beam on the ground.

A kind of gasping groan led them on, and in about fifty yards the beam of the torch picked up a dark form on the ground. As they approached, it turned a bloodied face towards them.

'By Timothy!' Temple breathed.

'Do you know him?'

'Yes.'

The injured man, dazzled by the torch, cringed away.

'Don't hit me. Please don't hit me again!'

'It's all right, Angus. No one's going to hurt you.'

'Who are—?' The man choked on the words, spitting blood.

'It's Paul Temple. We met at the police station.'

'Temp—' Ted Angus slumped back, exhausted by the effort to speak.

'Don't try to talk, Ted. Just lie still. We'll get help to you.'

'Ted Angus!' exclaimed Steve. 'Is that the man who—?'

'Yes! Ted Angus. The chap who drove the truck into Wyman's car.'

'Temple, listen . . .' The prone figure had raised his head. Temple handed Steve the torch and went down on one knee beside him, with a hand supporting his neck. 'This is important—'

'Yes, what is it?'

'Ask – ask Mrs Fletcher about – about—'

'Go on, Angus, I'm listening! Ask her about what? Dr Benkaray?'

'No.' Ted made a great effort and finally managed to deliver his message. 'Ask her about the coat.'

CHAPTER III

A Change of Mind

Though there were lights in the upstairs rooms at the back of the house and Temple could hear the bell pealing inside, there was still no sound of anyone coming to the door. For the third time he hammered on the knocker.

Thanks to the isolated light he had spotted before they heard Ted Angus's cries for help, Temple had been able to locate the two converted cottages a few hundred yards further down the lane. He had sent Steve back to the call-box on the road with instructions to 'phone the police and arrange for an ambulance to be sent as soon as possible. Angus had lost consciousness after making that cryptic statement about Mrs Fletcher and Temple's quick examination had convinced him that the little Scotsman stood little chance unless he received expert attention without delay.

He had his finger on the doorbell again when at last he heard a man's footsteps thumping across the hall. Instead of opening the door, he shouted from inside: 'Who's there? What do you want?'

'Open up,' Temple replied. 'It's urgent.'

'Who are you?'

'I tell you, it's urgent. Open the door!'

'Wait a minute,' the man growled angrily. Temple heard a bolt being drawn and a key turned in the lock.

The door opened at last to reveal a tall man of about forty with a hatchet face that was devoid of any emotion except suspicion. He was wearing an old woollen cardigan and a shirt buttoned to the neck, but no tie.

'Is this Dr Benkaray's house?'

'Yes,' the man admitted reluctantly. 'It is.'

Temple could tell now from the voice that this was the man he had spoken to on Dr Benkaray's Wimpole Street number, but he seemed far too dishevelled to be anyone's secretary.

'I must see the doctor. It's urgent.'

'The doctor isn't receiving visitors tonight.' The 'secretary' added, as an afterthought: 'She isn't very well.'

Temple heard a door opening at the end of the corridor. 'Don't you understand?' he insisted. 'This is an emergency. There's a man very badly hurt, probably dying. Will you please do as I say and fetch the doctor?'

'I've told you – she's not well.'

'Larry, what's this all about?'

Larry turned round at the woman's voice. His expression was that of a man who's only tried to do his best and been let down for his pains. Through the half-open door Temple could now see a tall, masculine-looking woman with greying hair. The face was intelligent; the features determined. Temple could see what Fred Harcourt had meant when he described her as striking-looking.

He put a foot in the door. 'Dr Benkaray?'

'Yes, I am Dr Benkaray.' Her voice had a faint mid-European quality, both in tone and pronunciation.

'My name is Paul Temple—'

'Temple!' Larry exclaimed. 'You never said your name was—'

'There is something wrong, Mr Temple?' Dr Benkaray cut across her secretary's protest.

'Yes, there's a man in your wood, he's very badly injured. When I left him he was—'

'Injured? In what way?'

'It looks to me as if he's been systematically beaten up—'

'Beaten up?' Larry objected. 'Are you trying to tell us—'

'Be quiet, Larry!' Dr Benkaray's voice was level but as cutting as a whiplash. 'I'll get my bag, Mr Temple. I'll be with you in a moment.'

'Do you know him, Doctor?'

'No.' Dr Benkaray straightened up from her crouching position and handed Temple back his torch. 'And I'm afraid there's nothing I can do for the poor fellow. He's dead.'

Temple took the torch, which was still switched on. He directed it at the ground, slightly away from Ted Angus's body. 'I thought it was hopeless.'

'But who is he?' Larry was still staring down at the inert and bloody form. 'And how the devil did he get here?'

'Have you heard anything suspicious this evening – any noise, for instance?'

'No, not a thing, have we, Doctor?'

'I've been resting.' Temple guessed that this was what the doctor had told Larry to say and so she had to stick to it. 'It's doubtful whether I should have heard anything, anyway. Neither myself nor Mr Cross – who is my secretary, by the way – know this man, Mr Temple. Can you tell us who he is?'

'His name is Ted Angus.'

The name apparently meant nothing to either of them.

'But what was he doing here?' Dr Benkaray asked.

'I don't know. That's something the police will have to find out.'

'Police?'

'Yes – I sent my wife to telephone for them as soon as we found him.'

'I see. And you, Mr Temple. What were you doing here?'

In the faintly reflected light he could just see her observant eyes quizzing him. 'I was on my way to see you, Dr Benkaray,' he said evenly.

'To see me?'

'I tried to make an appointment to see you at your Wimpole Street address, but Mr Cross here refused to . . .'

'That's right! Of course!' Larry made a big play of just remembering. 'You telephoned . . .'

'I telephoned,' Temple confirmed curtly.

'Why did you wish to see me, Mr Temple?'

Temple moved the beam of the torch so that it shone on the pale trunk of a birch tree and reflected a little more light upwards on to the doctor's face.

'I'm investigating the murder of Julia Kelburn. I think she was a patient of yours?'

'Yes, she was – for a little while.' Dr Benkaray had taken this question calmly. She shook her head sadly. 'She was a very sick girl, very sick.'

'You mean – mentally?'

'All the time she lived in great fear – a fear that dominated her.'

'A fear of what, exactly?'

'That is what I was trying to find out. I only saw her three times – perhaps four. I tried to get her to talk but always there was a barrier. I tried to break that barrier down, but it was no use.'

Conscious that she was under scrutiny, the doctor turned, moving a little further away from the corpse. Temple switched his torch off and the darkness of the wood closed round them. 'And what happened?'

'What usually happens in a case of that kind? She failed to turn up for an appointment and I never saw her again.'

'Dr Benkaray, you knew that Julia Kelburn had been murdered?'

'Yes – it was in the newspapers.'

'Then why didn't you inform the police that she had been a patient of yours?'

She turned towards him again. All he could see was a pale face in the darkness.

'What was the point? I had nothing to tell the police.'

'You could have told them about this phobia – about this fear of hers.'

'Do you think the police would have attached importance to it?'

'I think they might.' Temple paused, aware that Larry Cross was somewhere behind him. 'Dr Benkaray, tell me, did Julia Kelburn ever come to see you down here?'

'No. I don't see patients here – always in London. I bought this house so that I could get away from my patients and relax.'

Twigs crackled behind Temple. 'Which brings us to an interesting question, Mr Temple. How did you know the doctor had a place down here?'

The man's voice, which up till now had been defensive, had taken on an aggressive tone. Now that the spotlight had been taken off the horrifying spectacle of Ted Angus's body, he was recovering his old form.

'I made some enquiries.'

Temple's reply was met with silence by both doctor and secretary. The hoot of the owl came again but further away now. These human intruders seemed to have frightened all the natural wild life away from the place where a man had been beaten to death. It was with some relief that Temple heard the sound of vehicles slowing down at the end of the lane and several car doors banging.

'That'll be the police – probably with the ambulance.'

While Fred Harcourt stowed the Temples' suitcases in the boot of the Rover, Temple could hear Mrs Harcourt bidding Steve a fond farewell in the doorway of The Red Hart.

'I do hope you'll come and stay with us again, Mrs Temple.'

'I hope so, too,' Steve agreed tactfully. 'We've been very comfortable. I'm only sorry it wasn't for longer.'

'You want to come in the spring. It's lovely round here when the orchards are in bloom.'

Fred Harcourt, smiling at the sound of his wife's voice, carefully closed the lid of the boot.

'Mr Temple?'

'Yes, Fred?'

Speaking quietly, with an eye on his wife, Fred said: 'Do you think I could have a word with you before you leave?'

'Yes, of course.'

'We'll go into my office, sir.'

'Wait in the car, Steve,' Temple told his wife, who had at last managed to part from Mrs Harcourt. 'I won't be a minute.'

Giving a reassuring nod to Mrs Harcourt, Fred closed the door of his small office then picked a folded newspaper off the desk.

'I wanted you to take a look at this newspaper, Mr Temple. There's a piece here about this girl that was murdered. It says you're taking an interest in the case.'

'Yes, that's true.'

'Would you say that's a good photograph of her, Mr Temple?'

Temple took the paper and studied the small photograph beside a short news item.

'Well, I never met Julia Kelburn, but this looks a pretty good photograph, judging from the others I've seen. Why do you ask?'

'I've got a good memory for faces, Mr Temple,' Fred said. 'You sort of get the knack of it in this business.'

'You've seen this girl?'

Fred nodded and took the paper back. 'She spent the night here. It'd be about six months ago. I remember saying to the missus: "There's something strange about that girl," I said, "there's a sad look about her eyes."'

'Have you got her name in the register?'

Fred had already opened his register and turned back a few pages. He ran his finger down the column of names.

'That's another peculiar thing, she signed herself in as Julia Smith.'

Temple moved round beside him to study the handwriting. 'Julia Smith. London. For some reason she didn't give her real name.'

'That's what I said to the Missus when I saw the newspaper this morning. If there'd been a man with her, well, you expect that sort of lark then, but she was on her own – though a man did call for her early next morning.'

'Did you talk to her at all?'

'Only when she arrived. She stayed in her room all evening I sent down for four double whiskies – one at a time, of course. When I took 'em up, she looked to me as if she'd been crying. I'd half a mind to ask her if I could help her, but she didn't give me any opening.'

63

'You say a man called for her next morning?'

'Yes, soon after seven it was. I had to get up early to make out the bill, and I remember the Missus was upset because the girl wouldn't have any breakfast—'

'Did you see the man?'

'Yes, but I can't remember him as well as the girl.' Fred scratched his head. 'He was medium height, I think. Dark, curly hair, and spoke with a bit of an American accent.'

'What sort of terms were they on?'

Fred turned the corners of his mouth down and shook his head in a disappointed way.

'You might have thought he was her dad come to fetch her home—'

The Rover's petrol tank was nearly empty and according to Fred Harcourt the filling station was at the opposite end of Westerton from The Red Hart. The village street was crowded with the vehicles of farmers and country people who had come in to do their morning shopping. Temple drove slowly, still thinking about the information Fred Harcourt had given him. His description of the man who had come to collect Julia Kelburn had been vague, but it could just have fitted Mike Langdon.

'Did the local police say they knew Ted Angus?' Steve asked, busy with her own memories of the previous evening. They'd both been too tired to talk much before going to sleep.

'Well, the Inspector was inclined to be a bit cagey. I've an idea he's never tackled a murder case before. However, when we were at the station I managed to have a word with him. He's going to get in touch with Sir Graham, so I imagine Raine or somebody else at the Yard will take over. You said you'd got some information about Mrs Fletcher, Steve?'

'Yes, I managed to glean a few odds and ends when I went into the kitchen last night to persuade Mrs Harcourt to make us coffee. I felt bound to let her indulge in a bit of gossip, and as it happened it paid off.'

'Go on, Steve.'

'It seems that after she stopped being Dr Benkaray's daily, Mrs Fletcher bought this garage at the far end of the High Street. She's a widow but she's got a son – a boy of about twenty-two or three. They've made quite a go of the garage. Her son's a good mechanic, and Mrs Fletcher helps with the pumps and sells accessories and so on. But what intrigues all the locals is where she got the money to buy the garage in the first place.'

'Perhaps she borrowed it?' Temple suggested.

'A daily woman wouldn't find it easy to raise that sort of money. No, there's something very odd about it, Paul. According to Mrs Harcourt, the one thing Mrs Fletcher won't discuss under any circumstances is where she got the money from.'

'M'm. I expect the locals have some theory or other?'

'The most popular theory is that Benkaray played fairy godmother and bought the garage for Mrs Fletcher – but no one knows quite why she should.'

Half a mile ahead, just beyond the end of the High Street, Temple could see the oil company's sign hanging outside a service station and garage.

'Paul, did Dr Benkaray strike you as being the type of woman who would do that sort of thing?'

'I don't know, it's difficult to say. You know, this is very interesting about Mrs Fletcher, Steve – very interesting. Especially when one remembers what Ted Angus said.'

'Ask Mrs Fletcher about the coat . . .?'

'Yes. And that's exactly what we're going to do.'

A sign above the pumps at Fletcher's Garage informed customers, 'We serve you.' A young man of about twenty, clad in neat blue overalls, stepped up to the driver's window as Temple pulled in.

'Fill up – with four-star. And would you check the oil, water and battery, please?' As the attendant nodded and moved round to unscrew the filler cap, Temple told Steve: 'That must be young Fletcher. Keep him talking, Steve. I'm going to have a word with his mother.'

With the eyes of the pump attendant on him, Temple sauntered over to the little shop-cum-office at the back of the forecourt. A bell pinged as he opened the door. A woman of about fifty was standing behind the counter, checking a wad of five-pound notes. She was stoutish and quite smartly dressed. She looked capable and confident and Temple was not surprised that she had decided she could do better for herself than working for Dr Benkaray and her ill-tempered secretary. She gave him a welcoming smile and closed the notes in a drawer.

'Good morning,' Temple said. 'Do you sell cigars?'

'Over this side, sir.' She indicated a set of shelves beside the counter, stocked with cigarettes and packets of small cigars.

'Oh, yes! I'll have a packet of these, please – the Panatellas . . .'

'Thank you, sir.'

Temple handed her a five-pound note and watched her capable hands operate the cash register.

'Your change.' She glanced out at the Rover. 'Just driving down to the coast, sir?'

'No, as a matter of fact my wife and I spent the night here – at The Red Hart.'

'Oh.' She nodded non-committally. 'Not a bad little pub.'

'No, indeed.' Temple slipped the cigars and the change into his pocket. 'Mrs Fletcher, isn't it?'

'Yes, that's right,' she said, pleased to be known by name.

'Fred Harcourt mentioned you.'

'Oh . . .' Mention of the innkeeper's name was not an immediate recommendation.

'He said you used to work for Dr Benkaray.'

'Oh, did he?' The smile had been replaced by a frown.

'Yes,' Temple said, still casual and friendly. 'I'd heard of Dr Benkaray and happened to mention her name. Incidentally, while you were working for the doctor did you come across a man called Ted Angus?'

'No, I didn't.'

'You've heard the name before, I take it?'

'I can read,' she snapped. 'It's in the newspapers.'

'Angus was murdered last night – in the wood, not far from Dr Benkaray's place.'

'Yes, I know.'

'But you'd never heard of Angus – not until you'd read about him this morning?'

'No, I hadn't.' Mrs Fletcher drew in a long breath. 'Are you a newspaper man?'

'No.'

'Well, you ought to be – you're nosey enough for one!'

Behind Temple the bell pinged. The young man came in, wiping his hands on a cloth.

'Ma, could you . . .' He stopped when he saw the expression on his mother's face. 'Hello, something wrong?'

'This chap's askin' me a lot of questions, Bill. I don't know who he is but . . .'

'Well, I do!' Bill grinned. 'You're Paul Temple, aren't you?'

'That's right.'

'Thought so. Your photograph's on the back of a book I've been reading.' Bill gave Mrs Fletcher a nod and a wink. 'It's all right, Ma – he's nothing to do with the newspapers.'

Mrs Fletcher's expression relaxed to one of only slightly less hostility. 'Are you from the police, then?'

'No, but I'm helping the police to investigate a murder case; Julia Kelburn . . .'

'Oh, I read about her!' Mrs Fletcher exclaimed, relieved to be back on more familiar ground. 'Bit of a hot number, wasn't she?'

Temple did not respond to the innuendo. 'She was a patient of Dr Benkaray's.'

'Go on . . . Was she?' Bill said, with exaggerated surprise. 'Didn't know that, did you, Ma?'

'No, I didn't,' Mrs Fletcher agreed, a little baffled, but taking her cue. 'But then the doctor has hundreds of patients.'

Outside, at the pumps, a horn was being hooted, impatiently. Bill looked at Temple, still with that friendly smile fixed on his face. 'She was good to Ma, the doctor was.'

'That's Tom Eaton's van – go and see what he wants, Bill.'

'Okay.'

Bill, realising that his mother wanted to get rid of him, threw the cloth down and went out; the bell pinged unnecessarily as he opened the door. Temple leant an elbow casually on the counter.

'Mrs Fletcher, I don't want to make a nuisance of myself, but it might be worth your while to tell me one or two things.'

'What things?' she said defensively.

'My wife and I found Ted Angus last night. He'd been beaten up. Just before he died he mentioned your name.'

Her astonishment was unfeigned.

'Ted Angus did?'

'That's right.'

'You – you must be mistaken.'

'No, I wasn't mistaken.'

'Well, what did he say?'

Temple paused, watching her. 'He said: "Ask Mrs Fletcher about the coat."'

In her agitation she began to fiddle with the objects on the counter, moving the receipt pad, closing the lid of the rubber stamp pad, replacing the clip on a sheaf of repair slips.

'The coat? What coat? What was he talking about?'

'I don't know,' Temple said equably. 'I was hoping you'd tell me.'

'I don't know what this is all about,' she said, with a vigorous shake of the head. 'I don't know anyone called Angus. It wasn't me he was referring to – must have been another Mrs Fletcher.'

'I see. Very well.' Temple began to move away. 'I'm sorry to have troubled you.'

'Wait a minute! Have you said anything about this to the police or anyone?'

'No, not a word – and there's no reason why I should.' Temple reached into his pocket and brought out his wallet. 'Look – here's my card. If you should remember anything about Ted Angus or Julia Kelburn, just give me a ring.'

'Julia Kelburn? I never set eyes on the girl. She was never in these parts.'

She held the card at arm's length, screwing up her eyes to read the small print.

'According to Fred Harcourt she was. Well, if you remember anything give me a ring. It'll be worth your while, Mrs Fletcher, I assure you.'

*

The Temples had an early lunch at The Crown in Chislehurst, after which Temple put a call through to Scotland Yard. They were back in Eaton Square by three o'clock. When Charlie opened the door he seemed relieved to see them.

'You've got a visitor, Mr Temple.' Temple had already seen the hat and gloves on the hall table. 'It's a Mr Kelburn, sir. He's been here about twenty minutes.'

'Kelburn?' Temple gave Steve a puzzled look. 'Any other messages?'

'A Mr Langdon telephoned.' Charlie closed the front door. 'Twice, as a matter of fact. He said he'd ring back later.'

'Take this case, will you, Charlie? No,' Temple said, as Charlie reached for his own smaller suitcase, 'the big one.'

'Oh – very good, sir.' Charlie seized Steve's much bulkier case and grimaced as he felt its weight.

'Oh, and Charlie – I'm expecting Sir Graham Forbes. Show him into the sitting-room when he arrives.'

George Kelburn had been reading a book from Temple's shelves. He got up to put it back as he heard the door opening. Temple recognised the spine of one of his own novels, *The Tyler Mystery*. As his visitor turned towards him, Temple saw that his manner was totally different from the last time they had met, polite and controlled but unmistakably distant.

'Hello, Kelburn! Sorry to have kept you waiting, only my wife and I have been—'

'That's all right,' Kelburn said quickly. 'I apologise for intruding like this.'

'I don't think you've met my wife.'

'No, I haven't.' Kelburn bowed politely but did not offer to shake hands. 'Good afternoon, Mrs Temple.'

'How do you do, Mr Kelburn.' Steve's voice was a little cold. She had already sensed George Kelburn's mood, and did not ask him to sit down. Kelburn's next remark showed that she had been right.

'Temple, there's no point in beating about the bush. I'll get straight to the point. I've changed my mind.'

'Changed your mind? About what, exactly?'

'About the murder. About your investigation. I want you to withdraw from the case. Naturally, I'll pay any reasonable fee you decide to ask and any expenses which . . .'

'Wait a minute! Why have you changed your mind, Mr Kelburn?'

'I've thought about this and decided that there's nothing to be gained by further private investigation. It can't bring Julia back.'

Steve moved across to the window to adjust the curtains, which Charlie had pulled back carelessly that morning.

'No,' Temple said, 'but it might result in the murderer being brought to justice.'

Kelburn's stiff attitude relaxed a little and he let his shoulders droop. 'Yes, well – it's Julia I keep thinking about. It can't bring my daughter back. Naturally, I appreciate you feel some disappointment in losing a profitable assignment . . .'

'That's nothing to do with it,' Temple cut in with irritation. 'I make my money out of books, Kelburn—not other people's troubles. I'm working on this case simply because I became involved in it; there's no other reason.'

'But Mr Kelburn, surely you realise the police are bound to go on with their investigations?'

Kelburn turned towards Steve, who had moved out from behind the piano. 'Yes, Mrs Temple, I realise that. There's nothing I can do about the police, unfortunately.'

'And they'll expect you to co-operate,' she pointed out.

'I've already told the police all I know,' Kelburn said impatiently. 'There's nothing else I can say or do which

71

could possibly help them.' He turned back to Paul. 'I've given this matter a great deal of thought, Temple, and that's my decision.'

Temple shrugged. 'Very well, if that's your decision.'

'Now, don't be stupid about the financial aspect, I don't expect people to work for nothing. Send your account to my office in . . .'

'There won't be an account,' Temple interrupted, annoyed at being treated as if he were a minion on Kelburn's payroll. 'I started this investigation partly on your behalf. I shall continue it entirely on my own.'

'That's up to you, of course,' Kelburn said stiffly, straightening his jacket. 'But I can't undertake to give you any co-operation. In fact, I may be going abroad in the near future.'

'Very well.' Temple had begun to move towards the door, as a hint to Kelburn that the interview was finished.

'Sorry about this, Temple, but these decisions have to be taken.'

Temple ignored the man's attempt to end the meeting on a cordial note. 'I only hope this is one you won't regret. I'll see you out.'

'Thank you. Goodbye, Mrs Temple.' Again, Kelburn bowed stiffly. 'I'm glad to have met you.'

'It's been a pleasure,' Steve said, with icy insincerity.

Kelburn had not been gone five minutes when Sir Graham Forbes arrived, accompanied by Superintendent Raine. While Steve went to find Charlie and rustle up some tea, Temple took the two men into the sitting-room.

'Was that Kelburn we saw getting into his car?' Forbes asked.

'Yes, it was.'

Raine observed: 'He appeared to be in rather a bad mood.'

'Yes, I think he was. Excuse me a moment.'

Temple had heard the telephone ringing. As neither Steve nor Charlie seemed to be answering it, he went out into the hall to take the call.

It was Mike Langdon. He was going back to the States at the end of the week, he said, and wanted to see Temple before he left. As he was in the West End Temple suggested that he came round in an hour's time.

'You know where we are?'

'Yes. Eaton Square.'

'Right. I'll see you about five.'

In the sitting-room Sir Graham had made himself comfortable in an armchair, but Raine was prowling restlessly round the room.

'Yes, Kelburn was in a strange mood,' Temple said, picking up the conversation where they had left off. 'He asked me to withdraw from the case, Sir Graham. He says he doesn't want me to make any further investigations.'

'Why should he ask you to do that?'

'He didn't say why,' Temple said, sitting down in his own favourite chair, 'but I got the impression he was frightened.'

'Frightened of what?'

'I don't know.'

'You mean,' Raine said, 'you think someone's bringing pressure to bear on him?'

'Yes – or he's just plain frightened. Perhaps he knew Ted Angus . . .'

Raine finally decided to take a chair, but as always he chose a fairly upright one and sat perched on the forward edge. 'Tell us about Ted Angus, Mr Temple. What exactly happened last night?'

73

'Well, Steve and I went down to Westerton. You know why – I told you on the 'phone about Steve's visit to the dress shop and Dr Benkaray.'

Raine nodded.

'Well, after dinner we went for a drive. I wanted to take a look at Dr Benkaray's place. We parked the car and walked through the wood towards the house. Suddenly we heard a noise. It was Ted Angus – he'd been beaten up.'

Raine waited, but Temple did not embroider his account. 'Then what happened?'

'Steve went for the police and I fetched Dr Benkaray.'

'Did she recognise Angus?' Forbes asked.

'She said she'd never seen him before – and that went for the secretary, too.'

'The secretary?'

'Yes – an unfriendly character called Larry Cross.'

'Larry Cross.' Raine made a note of the name. 'Did the doctor ask you what you were doing in the wood?'

'Yes, she did. I said I was on my way to see her and that I wanted to question her about Julia Kelburn.'

'How did she react to that?'

'She wasn't particularly helpful. She said that Julia had some kind of a complex and during two or three brief interviews she'd failed to get to the bottom of it.'

'In other words – she stalled?'

'Yes,' Temple agreed.

'Well, we know Miss Kelburn's trouble. We probably know why she consulted the doctor.' Raine paused, but Temple did not oblige by asking the obvious question. 'Julia Kelburn was a drug addict.'

Temple did not show any great surprise. 'How did this come out?'

'Medical report on the post mortem,' Forbes explained. 'Incidentally, keep this to yourself, Temple.'

'Yes, of course.'

'We weren't completely surprised.'

'Have you told Kelburn?'

'Not yet,' said Raine. 'As soon as I've got a few more details from the doctor I'll make an appointment to see him.'

'I wonder if Kelburn knows and that's why he wants me to drop the case.'

'Yes, it's a possibility,' Forbes agreed. 'Let's face it, no one likes that sort of publicity.'

'I'll check on this Dr Benkaray, Mr Temple,' Raine promised, 'see what her background is.'

'Thank you, Superintendent. Incidentally, I meant to ask you – what about young Wyman? Is he all right now?'

'Yes, he went back to work last night,' said Raine. 'I dropped in on him just as he was finishing his act. He didn't say much, but I got the impression he thought that Angus had smashed into his car deliberately. That kid's scared, Mr Temple – if we could get on the right side of him I think he'd talk.'

'He's at The Hide and Seek, isn't he?' Temple said thoughtfully.

'That's right – in Leicester Square.'

The door had opened and when Forbes saw that it was Steve he immediately sprang to his feet. Temple and Raine followed his example in more leisurely fashion.

'What's all this about The Hide and Seek?' Steve wanted to know.

'We were talking about Tony Wyman, Steve,' said Forbes, adopting the courteous attitude he always showed towards Temple's wife.

'Oh, yes. How is he, Sir Graham?'

'He's all right now – he's back at work.'

'If you can call it work,' Steve remarked with a smile.

'It's work all right, Mrs Temple,' Raine told her earnestly. 'You should have seen him last night, the sweat was pouring off him.'

'I'd like you to have another talk with him, Temple,' Forbes said. 'Tonight, if possible.'

'Yes, it might be quite an idea. I'll get Charlie to book a table.'

'I take it I'm in on this, Paul?'

Steve had left the door open behind her and the rattle of a tea-trolley could be heard out in the hall.

'Yes, of course. You can wear your new dress.'

'I don't think it would be quite right for The Hide and Seek, darling. In any case, it hasn't arrived yet.'

Feeling Sir Graham's eyes fixed on her admiringly, Steve gave him a little smile then went to help Charlie by lifting the front of the trolley over the threshold.

'I don't think we can stop for tea, Steve,' Forbes protested, noting the scones and cakes on the lower shelf. 'You see . . .'

'Nonsense!' Steve brushed his excuses aside. 'Everything stops for tea in this house! Sit down, Superintendent, make yourself at home.'

Raine looked imploringly at Sir Graham, waiting for a cue. But the older and wiser man had accepted the inevitable.

'Sit down, Raine.'

Fortunately Langdon was late and so avoided butting in on the end of Steve's tea-party. Forbes and Raine had departed and the tea-trolley had been wheeled away when Charlie showed him in.

'Sorry I'm late, Temple. It took me a little longer to get here than I thought.'

'Sit down. Can I get you a drink?'

Langdon sank into a chair and passed a hand over his forehead. 'No, I won't have a drink, if you don't mind. Mr Temple, I wanted to see you about Kelburn. Quite frankly, I'm baffled. At one time he was quite determined to find out who murdered Julia, but now – I'm very sorry, Temple, but I'm afraid he wants you to withdraw from the case.'

'Yes, I know. Kelburn's been here. Why d'you think he's changed his mind? Has something happened?'

'Well,' Langdon said worriedly, 'it all seems to date from a letter he received this morning. I noticed him change colour the moment he read it.'

Temple had not sat down. He was standing in front of the fireplace looking at the American. 'Did he tell you what was in the letter?'

'No, he simply sent for me in the middle of the morning and told me he'd changed his mind about your investigating the case. I argued with him of course, but it was no use. It never is, once he's made up his mind.' Langdon shrugged his shoulders apologetically. 'I'm sorry, Temple.'

'That's all right, don't worry about me. But tell me, have you noticed anything else about Kelburn?'

'What do you mean?'

'Has his attitude changed in other directions – towards his wife, for instance?'

Langdon pondered for a few seconds before answering. 'Yes, I think it has. Up to a couple of days ago they seemed to get on very well together. Neither of them was very demonstrative but they appeared to enjoy each other's company. But on Monday night I happened to go downstairs fairly late to collect a book I was reading . . .' He stopped, hesitating before confiding to someone else what might be regarded as an invasion of privacy.

'Go on.'

'Well, they were in the lounge and shouting at each other as if all hell was let loose. I only heard the tail end of it, but boy, it was a humdinger of a row! I heard Kelburn say: "If you go on like this you'll finish up the same way as Julia."' Langdon looked Temple frankly in the eyes, his expression serious. That kind of shook me. Whether he meant Laura would finish up in the river, or whether he . . . Well, I don't know what he meant. But one thing I do know.' He grinned ruefully. 'I shall be mighty glad to get away from the Kelburn family and back to New York.'

'Yes, I can imagine that.' Temple smiled in response and then asked casually: 'Langdon, tell me, when were you last in England?'

'About six months ago,' Langdon answered easily. 'I came over to talk with Kelburn about a printing process.'

'You didn't by any chance visit a pub called The Red Hart at Westerton?'

'Westerton?' Langdon repeated the name without blinking. He thought for a moment, then shook his head. 'No, I don't think so. Where is that?'

'It's in Kent, about forty miles from London.'

'No, I've never been there. Might have passed through it, but I don't remember the place. Why do you ask?'

'Oh, nothing. I wondered, that's all.'

The Hide and Seek was very different from what Paul and Steve expected. The former night club had been converted to a jazz club, with tiered seats in a semi-circle round the residual patch of dance floor. There were small tables in front of the seats on which customers could put their drinks or at a later stage of the evening their plates of food. The Temples had half expected to find the place full of youngsters with dyed hair and kinky outfits, and had taken care to wear informal dress. To their surprise the seats were filled with serious, almost dedicated-looking people, though there was hardly a neck-tie to be seen. If Temple had not made Charlie book seats for them they would never have got in.

The group which had been hired to warm the audience up before Tony Wyman appeared – three blacks, three whites and one Vietnamese – were just finishing as they came in. The applause was muted but an air of expectancy built up as the stage was prepared for Tony Wyman. He was the star attraction of the evening. When he entered with his backing group of one double-bass, a drummer and a synthesiser, he was a totally different person from the nervous and awkward young man Temple had met. He was dressed in a suit of gleaming silver, which fitted him as tightly as a glove, and on stage he was as confident as an impresario.

Without preamble he took the microphone from its stand and gave the slightest of nods to his drummer. From the very first notes, Steve found herself unexpectedly impressed and when Tony Wyman began to sing she was moved in spite of herself. His hoarse, almost damaged voice gave a peculiar poignancy to the songs and when he worked up to a crescendo he seemed to be forcing the words out with a superhuman effort and with acute physical pain. As Raine had rightly remarked, he was putting everything he had got into the performance and soon the perspiration was glistening on his face. For forty-five minutes he held the audience spellbound and when he took his last bow and went off there was a storm of applause, foot-stamping and whistles. But Tony Wyman gave no encore. After a decent interval the loudspeakers began to dispense the latest hit tunes, the multi-coloured lights started to sweep round the room and the first couples went down on to the space cleared for dancing.

Steve declined Temple's suggestion that they should take to the floor. 'I don't feel like dancing, Paul. This music seems so banal after that. I think what I'd like is a good strong whisky.'

Half an hour after Wyman's act had ended Temple was beginning to wonder if he had received the note he had sent round to his dressing-room, but at last he appeared. In the dim and distorted light hardly anyone recognised the inconspicuous young man now dressed in jeans and a short leather jacket. He slid into the seat beside Temple.

'Sorry to have kept you, Mr Temple. I had to make two telephone calls and then my agent popped in and I couldn't get rid of him. He's still waiting for me, as a matter of fact, so I can only spare you a couple of minutes.'

'That's all right. Oh, I don't think you know my wife.'

'No, I don't.' Wyman nodded perfunctorily at Steve. 'Hello.'

'We enjoyed your performance.' She gave him a warm smile.

'Thanks, but it wasn't so hot tonight. Wasn't feeling too good.'

'I expect you're still feeling a bit shaky,' Temple suggested.

'Yes, I am. The doc says I'm okay, but I don't feel it!'

'I suppose you read about the man who crashed into us – Ted Angus?'

'Yes.' Wyman took a break from biting his nails. 'Is that right what they said in the paper – that he was murdered?'

'Yes. He was beaten up and left for dead.'

Wyman's face was a deathly colour and the green and blue lights flashing across it made him look even more unhealthy. Temple leant towards him so that his voice would be audible against the boom of the loudspeakers.

'Angus smashed into your car quite deliberately. He was out to get one of us. I think it was you, Tony.'

'Thanks.' Wyman made a feeble attempt at a laugh. 'You've made my night!'

'You were going to tell me something just before the accident happened. What was it?'

'I don't remember,' Wyman said quickly.

'Please try to remember, because . . .'

'I've told you, I don't remember!'

'Was it about Dr Benkaray?'

'I've never heard of any Dr Benkaray.'

'Now don't be stupid, Tony. It was you who told me about her. Incidentally, Ted Angus was found two hundred yards from the doctor's cottage. Did you know that?'

Shaken, Wyman jerked his eyes towards Temple. 'No. No, I didn't.'

'Well, he was.'

Wyman had half risen, his eyes questing around as if he was not sure where the exit to the dressing-rooms was. 'Look, Mr Temple, my manager's told me to keep my mouth shut. He says I've done too much talking and I think he's right. I don't know nothin' about this bloke Angus or about Dr Benkaray or about Julia Kelburn – I just know nothin'.'

'All right, Tony. But if you get into trouble – the sort of trouble that manager of yours can't get you out of – give me a ring.'

'I don't know why you should talk to me like this, Mr Temple. I shan't get into trouble.'

Wyman had completely forgotten the existence of Steve. Without saying goodbye he quickly snaked between the seats and tables, pushed his way round the dancers on the floor and disappeared through the door at the back of the stage.

'Well, what do you make of him, Steve?'

Steve was staring wistfully at the door which had swung shut behind the singer.

'My word, he's a frightened young man if ever I saw one.'

Steve had been silent as their taxi dropped them in Eaton Square and she was still thoughtful as they waited for the lift to come down from the fifth floor.

'Paul, that man we saw driving the red car at Hyde Park Corner. What did you say his name was?'

'Larry Cross. Dr Benkaray's secretary.'

During a momentary hold-up at the western end of Piccadilly, Temple had glanced across as a scarlet Alfa-Romeo had pulled up beside them. He had immediately leant back out of sight. Unless both Mrs Kelburn and Larry Cross had a double they were driving home together at one o'clock in the morning. Steve, following his glance, had made an exclamation of surprise before Temple pulled her back. Then their own taxi had jerked forward.

'I've remembered where I saw him before. It was at the airport—'

'The airport?'

'Yes. He was the man in uniform, the airport official I told you about. He had a moustache then, but it was the same man. I'm sure of it.'

'How can you be sure, Steve? You were in a pretty bad state that night.'

'Well, I was still compos mentis when he first spoke to me,' Steve said, stepping into the lift.

Temple checked his watch before he put his latchkey in the lock. It was ten to one.

'I expect Charlie's in bed,' Steve whispered.

'No, I'm not, Mrs Temple,' said Charlie, emerging from the kitchen with a self-righteous air. 'The 'phone's been going for the last hour but every time I answered it they rang off.

I was just making myself a nice cup of tea. Would you like a cup, sir?'

'No, thank you. I'm more in the mood for a whisky and soda. What about you, Steve?'

But Steve was more interested in a patterned box tied up with coloured ribbon which was standing on the hall table.

'What's this box, Charlie?' Then her face lit up with anticipation. 'Oh, it's my dress – from Daphne Drake's!'

'Yes, a young lady delivered it just after you left. Shall I put it in your dressing-room, Mrs Temple?'

'No, Charlie. I'll take it myself.'

'Are you going to have a nightcap, Steve?' asked Temple.

'Yes, pour me a brandy, darling – just a tiny one. I'm going to try my dress on.'

'What, at this hour of the morning?'

'I'll be along in a minute. And pour yourself a stiff one, Paul. You'll need it when I tell you what I paid for the dress.'

Clutching her precious box Steve disappeared along the passage that led to the bedroom and the two dressing-rooms. Charlie cast his eyes to heaven at the unpredictability of women.

Temple laughed and sauntered into the sitting-room. Taking his time he took out the last of the Panatellas he had bought from Mrs Fletcher and lit it. He switched on the radio, but the jazz music it was churning out sounded trite after what he had heard at The Hide and Seek. He went across to the drinks cupboard, took out a couple of brandy glasses and reached for the bottle of Courvoisier. He was just pouring the first glass when the telephone began to ring. Although he knew what time it was he automatically glanced at his watch. Five minutes to one in the morning! He carefully poured a second glass, put the cork back in the bottle and replaced it in the cupboard. Then he went across and picked up the receiver.

When he heard the bleeps and knew that the call was coming from a pay 'phone he was certain that someone had dialled a wrong number.

'Hello,' he said, as the coins went in. 'Hello?'

'Mr Temple?' It was a woman's voice, one he had heard before.

'Yes, speaking. Who is that?'

'It's—it's Margo.'

'Margo?' Temple repeated. He had identified the voice now. It was Mrs Fletcher, the owner of the garage at Westerton.

'Mr Temple,' she said urgently, but still trying to disguise her voice. 'Don't let your wife open that box—'

'Which box? Do you mean the one from the dress shop—?'

'Yes! Don't let her touch it, Mr Temple. Whatever you do don't let her open it—'

Temple did not wait to hear any more. He banged the receiver down and dashed for the door. As he reached the hall he was already shouting at the top of his voice: 'Steve! Don't open the box—'

He was almost at the end of the passage and was close to the door of the bedroom when he felt a blast and heard ahead of him a loud explosion. Steve's scream reached him against a background of crashing china and breaking glass.

CHAPTER IV

Bill Fletcher's Story

'Drink this, Steve.'

'What is it?'

'Brandy. It'll do you good. You're sure you're not hurt, nothing broken?'

'No. I seem to be all in one piece – thanks to you, darling.'

Temple had rushed into the bedroom to find Steve lying face downwards on the big double bed, perfectly still. But at the sound of his agonised cry she had scrambled up and rushed into his arms. Charlie, who had run into the room a few seconds after Temple, had been despatched to fetch brandy and was now standing watching his master and mistress with concerned eyes. Temple had his arm protectively round his shivering wife's shoulders.

'Now, tell me what happened, Steve.'

Steve took a sip of brandy and stared into her devastated dressing-room. The dressmaker's box had vanished and a circle of destruction radiated outwards from the dressing-table where it had stood.

'I took the box into the dressing-room and started to undo the ribbon. I had just lifted the lid when I heard you shouting. I started for the bedroom and had just got to the door when the thing exploded. I felt myself pushed from behind as if by some giant hand and found myself taking a dive on to the bed. Thank goodness you shouted, darling!'

Steve tossed back the brandy and handed the glass to Charlie.

'Shall I fetch you some more, Mrs Temple?'

'Thank you, Charlie. I think it's doing me good. Oh, Paul! Just look at the dressing-room! Look at the window!'

'Never mind about the dressing-room. As long as you're all right—'

'What made you shout like that?'

'A woman telephoned. She warned me not to let you open the parcel—'

'A woman? What woman?'

'She said her name was Margo,' Temple said slowly, 'but I'm pretty sure it was Mrs Fletcher.'

'Mrs Fletcher who owns the garage? Whoever it was I'm glad she telephoned. Someone was trying to kill me, Paul!'

He felt her shiver. A cold draught was feeling its way in through the shattered window. 'Let's go along to the sitting-room. Charlie and I can clear up this mess later.'

Charlie, on his way along the passage with the brandy bottle, did an about turn and took it into the sitting-room. As Steve and Paul came in he was switching on the electric fire and drawing the curtains.

'Paul,' Steve was saying, 'I can't for the life of me think why anyone at Daphne Drake's should do a thing like that! After all, they'd be the first to be questioned.'

Temple agreed. He was still shaken by the narrowness of Steve's escape, and very angry. 'Let's think back a bit. It was

Laura Kelburn who sent us to Daphne Drake's in the first place. She said that Julia bought most of her clothes there.'

'Yes, that's right.' Steve turned a pale and startled face towards him. 'But surely you don't think Laura had anything to do with tonight?'

'I wouldn't be too sure,' Temple said grimly. 'After all, what was she doing with Larry Cross, Dr Benkaray's so-called secretary? And why did she make two telephone calls to us and then flatly deny that she made them?'

Steve sat down on the sofa and Temple sat beside her. He felt a need to stay very close to her.

'There's your brandy, Mrs Temple.' Charlie, with his best bedside manner, handed her a replenished glass.

'Thank you, Charlie.'

'If I remember rightly,' Temple said, 'you told me you bumped into Laura when I was in America?'

'That's right. Twice.'

'Twice? I didn't realise that. What happened?'

'Well, I met her at Harrods on the Saturday morning – the day after you left. We had coffee together. About three weeks later she 'phoned and said she wanted to see you.'

'And you said I was in the States?'

'That's right. A few days later I bumped into her again and naturally mentioned the 'phone call. You know what happened – she said she hadn't made it.'

'Yes.' Temple reflected for a moment. 'Steve, the first time you met her – what did you talk about?'

'Oh – old times. Fleet Street, the usual gossip.'

'And nothing particular happened on that occasion – nothing unusual, I mean?'

'No, nothing, darling.' Steve shook her head, then added as an afterthought, 'Oh, she asked me to post a letter for her.'

'Post a letter?'

'Yes.' Steve was surprised at the sharpness of the question. 'I happened to mention I was going to a nearby post office to buy some stamps. She said she had a letter she'd forgotten to post and would I post it for her.'

'Who was the letter to?'

'I don't remember,' Steve said, laughing. 'Paul, why are you looking so serious?'

Temple's thoughts were far away. 'What's that, Steve?'

'I said, why the serious expression?'

'I was just thinking . . .' Temple abruptly stood up. 'I was just thinking I'd have a brandy myself, Steve.'

In spite of the standard paintwork, modern fittings and official furniture, Sir Graham Forbes had stamped his own personality on the large office he occupied on the sixth floor of the headquarters of the Metropolitan Police. He had brought in his own mahogany, leather-topped partners' desk and three comfortable chairs that might have come from a London club. One wall was reserved for Ackerman prints of his old school and Cambridge college. On another was displayed a large-scale map of London, sub-divided into the various divisions and studded with pins of half a dozen different colours. Prominent on his desk was a signed photograph of the Queen and Prince Philip. The broad windows looked out on Victoria Street and commanded a view towards Westminster Cathedral on one side, to the Abbey and Houses of Parliament on the other.

Temple had preferred to remain standing up, enjoying the view of the city in the morning sunlight. Sir Graham was behind his desk and Raine was in one of the club armchairs. As it was virtually impossible to sit on the edge of them he had been forced to lean back, but he looked awkward and uncomfortable.

'But who did you see, Raine?' Forbes pressed the Superintendent. 'Was it the proprietor, or just the woman who runs the shop?'

'The manageress, Sir Graham,' Raine answered patiently. 'They called her Miss Elsie.'

'Yes,' Temple put in. 'That's the woman who attended to Steve.'

'She had a pretty plausible explanation, I must admit. Apparently, they were going to deliver the parcel themselves and then at about four p.m. a young woman called and said she had been asked by Mrs Temple to collect the dress. Naturally, they thought the woman was bona fide.'

'So they handed it over.'

'Yes. And then, of course, the girl switched parcels.'

'Did you get a description of this girl?'

'Well, I did my best,' Raine said defensively, 'but they were all pretty vague. I suppose that's understandable, it's a very busy shop. They thought she was about twenty-seven or eight, average height, dark-coloured hair. No distinctive features.'

'No distinctive features!' Forbes exploded. 'Ye gods, the times we hear that one! You know, I don't think we'll get anywhere with this investigation until we find the motive. And I don't mean the motive for what happened last night, but the motive for the murder.'

Temple nodded his agreement.

'Well, surely the most likely lead is the fact that Julia Kelburn was a drug addict, sir.'

'You've consulted the Narcotics people, of course?'

Raine was a little nettled at Temple's implication that he might have left this stone unturned. 'Oh, they're on to it, Temple. But they haven't come up with anything – not yet, at any rate.'

'What about this doctor,' Forbes said, 'Benkaray?'

'I saw her yesterday, sir. I went down to Westerton to have a word with the local people. Dr Benkaray seems to be genuine. She's been practising in town for the last ten years. But I didn't get much information out of her about Julia Kelburn. She was very cagey.'

'Did you meet her so-called secretary, Larry Cross?' Temple enquired tentatively.

'Yes, I did. Now he's a tough egg, if ever I saw one. Doesn't look a bit like my idea of a doctor's secretary.'

'Nor anyone else's. We saw him last night when we were returning from The Hide and Seek. He was with Laura Kelburn. They were in a red sports Alfa-Romeo together. Cross was driving. Steve thinks that Cross was the man who spoke to her at London Airport – the phoney official.'

'You mean,' Raine said eagerly, 'she'd be able to identify him?'

'Yes, but don't do anything yet, Raine. Steve may be mistaken and we don't want . . .'

Temple paused as there came a knock on the door at the same instant as it opened. A uniformed sergeant came half into the room.

'Excuse me, sir. Mr Kelburn to see you.'

'Oh, yes.' Forbes swivelled his chair and stood up. 'Show him in, Sergeant.'

'Did you send for Kelburn, Sir Graham?' Raine said, caught slightly on the wrong foot.

'Yes, I did. I think it's only fair we tell him about this new development.'

'You mean the heroin?' Raine said doubtfully.

'Yes. He's a right to know, and in any case he may be able to help us.'

Before Raine could express any contrary point of view the door was opened again. The sergeant leaned back against it to let the visitor pass.

'Mr Kelburn, sir.'

Raine struggled out of the slippery chair as Forbes crossed the room to meet Kelburn.

'Come in, Mr Kelburn. My name is Forbes. I think you've met Superintendent Raine and Mr Temple.'

'Yes,' Kelburn said grimly. 'I have.'

'Please sit down.'

Kelburn looked older and more strained, but he had dressed carefully in a grey pin-striped suit and had lost none of his confident arrogance. He stared levelly at Temple.

'I'd rather stand, if you don't mind. I didn't expect to find you here, Temple.'

'I had an appointment with Sir Graham. I'm just about to leave.'

'There's no reason for you to leave – so far as I'm concerned.' He turned to Forbes, assuming that his comment would be taken as an order. 'What is it you want, Sir Graham?'

'Certain information has reached us concerning your daughter – we thought it only fair that . . .' Forbes hesitated in the face of Kelburn's uncompromising stare. '. . . that you should be made aware of it.'

'What information? What are you referring to?'

'I'm afraid it's been established, Mr Kelburn, that your daughter took heroin.'

Kelburn made no comment and his expression did not change.

'You don't seem very surprised.'

'No, I'm not.'

'You knew?'

'Yes.'

Raine took a couple of steps forward, so that he would come into Kelburn's field of vision. 'How long have you known, sir?'

'About two or three days. That's why I tried to stop your investigation, Temple. I didn't want you to find out about Julia. I thought if you found out that she was on heroin, then the Press would get on to it and, well, the whole unsavoury business would be revived again – the murder and everything.'

'Who told you your daughter was a drug addict, sir?'

'I do wish you wouldn't use that phrase, Superintendent!' Kelburn said, with his first show of emotion. 'No one told me, I – I sensed it.'

'Just sensed it?' Raine looked dubious.

'Mr Kelburn,' Temple said, 'part of the time Julia mixed with people of her own class, the sons and daughters of fairly wealthy parents.'

Kelburn nodded warily.

'But at other times she used to associate with quite a different type of person, people on the fringe of the underworld . . .'

'Nonsense!'

'It isn't nonsense,' Temple insisted gently. 'It's true. Your daughter took heroin, therefore she got the heroin from somewhere. Now, the point is – where from? It's unlikely that her respectable friends would peddle the stuff, so it's my guess—'

'No one's interested in your guesses, Temple,' Kelburn said offensively.

Temple refused to be ruffled by the man's outburst. 'On the contrary, I'll make a guess that will interest *you*. Interest you very much.'

Kelburn was curious in spite of himself. 'What do you mean?'

'I don't believe you just sensed that your daughter was an addict, that's absurd. My guess is that someone wrote you a letter and told you in plain language that your daughter was hooked on heroin.' Temple's eyes were fixed on Kelburn. 'Am I right?'

Kelburn hesitated, then turned to Forbes. 'I think I will sit down, Sir Graham, after all.'

'Of course.'

Kelburn took one of the armchairs and rubbed one side of his forehead with two fingers. Forbes, out of politeness, took the chair opposite him but Raine and Temple remained standing.

'Who wrote the letter?' Temple moved round in front of Kelburn, pressing home his advantage.

'A girl – a very old friend of Julia's.' Kelburn spoke wearily, his eyes on the carpet. 'Fiona came to the house quite often. She was a nice girl, highly respectable, and she intensely disliked Julia's more rackety friends. She was always trying to persuade Julia to live a more useful life, to – well – settle down.' Kelburn, apparently with great effort, lifted his head. 'After the murder Fiona wrote me a letter, Temple, saying that I'd made a mistake in asking you to investigate the case. She said you were bound to discover that Julia was taking heroin and the inevitable consequences of such a discovery would be weeks of unsavoury publicity.'

'And you believed that?' Temple said drily.

'Of course! It's the truth. Temple, be honest – you know damn well it's the truth! Once the newspapers get hold of a story like this, they just never let go.'

'Who is this girl, Fiona?' Raine demanded. 'What's her surname?'

'I'm sorry, I'm not prepared to divulge that.'

'But you must divulge it!' Raine told him. 'We've got to question the girl, ask her . . .'

'No one's questioning her! No one's seeing her!' Kelburn thumped the arm of the chair with a clenched fist. 'Whatever happens, I'm not having Fiona subjected to a police cross-examination. The girl wrote me the letter simply out of kindness and I haven't the slightest intention . . .'

'Mr Kelburn, I see your point of view and I appreciate it,' Forbes said quietly, 'but you don't understand – you've got to tell us who this girl is. We're investigating a murder case.'

'I'm sorry, Sir Graham, I've made up my mind about this. If it hadn't been for Temple here, I wouldn't even have told you about the letter.'

Raine spoke in his most official voice. 'I suppose you know that it's an offence to withhold information from the police, sir?'

'Yes, I know.'

Kelburn leant back in his chair and crossed his legs. The smile he gave Raine was almost friendly.

'But I'm still going to withhold it, Superintendent.'

When Steve arrived home from her appointment with the hairdresser Charlie greeted her with a message from Temple. He wanted her to pick him up at his club as soon as possible after she returned.

'He said to bring the Rover, Mrs Temple.'

'The Rover? I wonder where we're going.' She smiled. 'No more parcels been delivered, Charlie?'

But Charlie did not see any humour in that remark. 'When will they be redecorating your dressing-room?'

'Just as soon as I've chosen a wallpaper. And I want to persuade Mr Temple that we might as well have the bedroom done at the same time.'

Charlie nodded and permitted himself a smile.

At the club Steve stayed with the car, which was on a double yellow line, while the porter went in to tell Temple she was there. He came out holding a manila envelope, which he handed to Steve as he slipped into the driving seat.

'Mm,' he murmured, glancing appreciatively at her hair. 'Very nice.'

'Where are we going, darling?'

'Down to Westerton, but we shan't be staying the night.'

'Just as well, as I haven't brought a suitcase. What's in the envelope, Paul?'

'Oh, some photographs.' Temple checked the traffic before pulling out. 'They were taken for me yesterday and delivered to the club.'

'Photographs of what?'

'Mike Langdon. They're not bad, considering they were taken in the street without his knowing.'

'You're going to show them to Fred Harcourt at The Red Hart? You know, I've got a sort of intuition he was the man who called for Julia Kelburn that morning.'

Temple chuckled. 'I was wondering when that good old intuition would start to work—'

'You can laugh, but I've been right before.'

'Yes. Well, get your intuition to work on Mrs Fletcher. Tell me how she fits into the picture.'

'I wish I could,' Steve said, puzzled. 'I just can't make head or tail of Mrs Fletcher. But, if it was her on the 'phone, I'm more than grateful to her.'

'It was Mrs Fletcher all right. She'd been ringing for an hour, waiting till one of us answered. That's another reason I want to go down to Westerton.'

Steve waited till Temple had negotiated the traffic in Trafalgar Square before broaching the subject that was on her mind.

'Darling, the decorator came to look at my dressing-room this morning. He was very on the ball. He suggested that if we're doing the dressing-room we might as well do the bedroom as well. He showed me some very nice wallpapers—'

Temple listened without comment as she deployed her argument and she was concentrating on her theme so hard that she did not at first notice that he had slowed down and was trying to read the names of the side-streets.

'But Paul, this isn't the way we usually go to the coast.'

'I know. But I have a call to make first. Ah, here we are, Northcote Street. Now look out for Monte Carlo Mansions. It should be on the right.'

'Who on earth lives at Monte Carlo Mansions?'

'Who do you think would live at Monte Carlo Mansions? Mr Tony Wyman, of course.'

Temple made Steve wait in the car while he went inside the modern block of flats. She whiled away the time by studying the photos of Mike Langdon and listening to a talk on Radio 4. Temple was only gone ten minutes and when he came out he was looking very pleased with himself.

'Well,' Steve demanded, 'what's so funny?'

'Wyman. He spun me a tale about being a very busy man, but he was still in his pyjamas and it's after midday.'

'Well, he does work very late—'

'Yes, he was pretty bleary-eyed. I felt a bit brutal leaning on him as I did. He tried to make out that he did not know Julia was on heroin, but when I told him that his story did not tally with Fiona's he was so rattled that he let out her surname.'

'And what is her surname?'

'Scott. Fiona Scott. And he also let slip that she lives in Brighton. Apparently Julia took him down there to see her one Sunday and they didn't exactly hit it off.'

Temple had turned the car and was heading back towards the Old Kent Road.

'You know, I can't help feeling sorry for Wyman. He's dead scared of me, but I can't persuade him that I'm not trying to pin anything on him. Do you fancy lunching at that pub in Chislehurst again?'

It was still early afternoon when they reached Westerton. There was less traffic in the sleepy village street than on the morning they had first visited Fletcher's Garage. As he approached the filling station Temple saw a Peugeot estate at one of the pumps in the forecourt and a familiar figure standing beside it talking to Bill Fletcher. The latter was holding the nozzle of the pipe in the petrol tank of the Peugeot. A woman was sitting in the passenger's seat.

Instead of pulling in at the pumps, Temple drove the Rover into the service bay where the air-line and water pipe were available for customers and parked it facing the wall.

'Don't turn round, Steve. That's Larry Cross over there and I think it's Dr Benkaray sitting in the car. Just our luck. I don't want him to realise that you've recognised him.' Temple opened the door. 'Back me up if I bring Bill Fletcher over to look at the car.'

Temple sauntered over to the pumps. Bill Fletcher was just withdrawing the nozzle from the tank.

'Good afternoon,' Temple greeted Bill, ignoring Larry Cross. 'I'm afraid my car's giving me a spot of trouble and I wondered if you could have a look at it for me?'

'Be with you in a minute, sir.' Bill gave Temple his friendly smile and screwed the filler cap on the petrol tank of the Peugeot.

'Thank you.' Temple was moving away when the window of the Peugeot was wound down and a face peered up at him. 'Good afternoon, Mr Temple.'

Temple turned, feigning surprise. 'Oh, hello, Doctor!'

'What are you doing in this part of the world?' Dr Benkaray made the enquiry sound almost like an accusation.

'I'm on my way to the coast, and the wretched car's gone all temperamental. Is this chap any good?'

'Yes, I think he's a good mechanic.'

'We had a friend of yours down here yesterday, Temple,' Larry Cross chipped in, with his harsh, aggressive voice. 'Superintendent Raine.'

'Yes, so I believe.'

'Asked a lot of damn silly questions. He seems to think there's a connection between the Ted Angus murder and the Kelburn affair. I can't imagine why.'

'Well, perhaps you haven't got sufficient imagination, Mr Cross.'

'What do you mean?' Cross demanded belligerently.

'Do you think there's a connection, Mr Temple?' Dr Benkaray asked quickly.

'Yes, I do.'

'Well, tell us – what is the connection?' said Cross. 'We're always keen to learn.'

'You should have asked the Superintendent that question.'

'We did,' Dr Benkaray said, 'but unfortunately he didn't enlighten us.'

Bill Fletcher had checked the figure on the pump's indicator and was waiting for a chance to break into the conversation. 'That's nine pounds seventy, Doctor.'

'Charge it to my account, will you? Oh, and Bill . . .'

'Yes, Doctor?'

'Ask your mother to telephone me when she gets back.'

'Yes.' Bill nodded respectfully. 'I'll do that.'

Larry Cross walked round the car and clumsily inserted

his body behind the wheel. All his movements were violent and badly co-ordinated. The starter yammered and the engine revved excessively as he put his foot on the accelerator.

Dr Benkaray started to crank her window up. 'Goodbye, Mr Temple. No doubt we shall meet again some time.'

'Goodbye, Doctor.'

Temple stood, watching the car as Larry Cross forced his way into the road in front of an oncoming lorry.

'Having trouble with your car, Mr Temple?'

'What?' Temple reluctantly took his eyes from the receding car and turned towards Bill Fletcher. 'Oh, no, I wanted to talk to you.'

'Talk to me? What about?'

'About your mother.'

Bill's face became serious. He stared at Temple, trying to read his expression, then glanced towards the road to make sure no other cars were pulling in.

'Okay – let's go in the office.'

The friendly bell pinged as Bill led the way into the small office-cum-shop. Temple saw at once that there was no one behind the counter and the litter of papers, receipts, cheques and envelopes on it seemed to indicate that Bill was coping single-handed with the day's business.

Mrs Fletcher was up in town for the day, Bill explained, visiting Aunt Gladys. Seeing Temple's disappointed expression, he asked: 'Did you specially want to see her? Is there anything I can do?'

'It's a rather personal matter,' Temple hedged. Then, realising that Bill really wanted to be helpful, he said: 'I heard Dr Benkaray ask you to get your mother to 'phone her. Are they close friends?'

'I suppose you could say that. Mother used to work up at her place, and when we moved down here the doctor became one of our best customers.'

Temple noticed the reservation in the young man's answer. He asked bluntly: 'Do you like the doctor?'

'She's been very good to Mother.'

'That wasn't what I asked you.'

'I'd sooner keep my likes and dislikes to myself, if you don't mind, Mr Temple.' Bill's face had closed up and the helpful smile had gone.

'That's sensible of you.' Temple kept his voice friendly. 'It's just that your mother did me a very great favour and I'd like to repay her.'

'My mother did you a favour?'

'Yes. An attempt was made on my life, or rather on my wife's – and your mother 'phoned and tipped me off.' Temple smiled. 'Otherwise we might not be here today.'

'This is news to me,' said Bill, genuinely surprised. 'Are you sure it was my mother who telephoned you?'

'I'm pretty sure.'

'Well, Mother wouldn't expect any money, you know – even if she did do you a favour.' Bill spoke with a certain defensive aggressiveness.

'I wasn't thinking of that,' Temple told him. 'I had a feeling she was in some kind of trouble and it occurred to me that I might be able to help her in some way. I've a certain amount of influence, you know.'

'Yes, I know, Mr Temple.' Bill was regretting his momentary sharpness and trying to make up for it. 'I've heard a great deal about you and I've always thought . . . But how did you know my mother was in trouble?'

Bill did not seem to realise that he had made an important

admission and Temple's face did not betray the fact that his very tentative theory had been confirmed.

'Bill, why don't you tell me about it? I give you my word I'll treat the whole thing in confidence.'

He saw Bill hesitate, trying to make up his mind and then, to his frustration, a car pulled in at the pumps. He waited while the young man went out, served his customer, received payment and gave change. But when he came back Bill had made up his mind.

'Well, it's like this, Mr Temple,' he said, as if there had been no interruption. 'When I was a lad we used to live at Little Weston, about two miles away. Dad died when I was sixteen, and Mother went out to work. There wasn't much money, but I got a job in the garage at Little Weston. When I was nineteen we came to live here. Mother got this job with Dr Benkaray and she managed to fix me up at Perrymount Engineering, helping to repair tractors and things. I always wanted a garage of my own, as long as I can remember, but there was never any money.'

He paused as a van slowed on the road outside, its left-hand indicator blinking, but it passed the garage and turned up a lane beyond it.

'Well – we went on steadily enough, and then Mother started going to the doctor's afternoons as well as mornings, sometimes evenings as well. Then, after about two years, she came home one night and said she'd finished at the doctor's and was buying this garage which had just come on the market. She got it cheap enough, too, on account of putting down the ready.'

'D'you think your mother saved enough money to buy the garage?' As there were no chairs on the customers' side of the office Temple had leant back with his elbows supported on the counter.

'No, she couldn't have saved a quarter of it. I asked her where the rest came from but she'd never let on. Said she'd managed to raise a loan, and it was her business.' Bill shook his head. 'But in spite of everything, Mr Temple, Mother isn't happy. I'm sure she isn't. Don't ask me why, but she isn't.'

'You said she's in London at the moment?'

'Yes, she's always popping up to town these days to see her sister – that's my Aunt Gladys. They've never been as friendly. In the old days Mother used to say they only met at weddings and funerals.'

'You sound a bit suspicious of your aunt?'

'Oh, no, it isn't that, but after one of these trips I saw a theatre programme sticking out of Mother's handbag. It was from the Theatre Royal at Brighton.'

'She could have gone to Brighton. Perhaps she took your aunt there.'

'Then why didn't she tell me about it? At one time she used to tell me everything.'

'Well, if she isn't seeing your aunt she's obviously seeing someone on these trips of hers. You have no idea who it is?'

Bill stared out of the window, his brow puckered as he dug into his memory. 'There was one chap – he came to the house late one night, about two months ago.'

'Can you tell me anything about him?'

'Mother and he had a row. She thought I was asleep in bed, but when I heard voices I went to the top of the stairs. They were standing in the hall arguing with each other. I'd never seen the man before but I think he was an American . . .'

'Did you see him – clearly enough to recognise him again?'

'I think so. Yes, I'm sure I would.'

Temple was already pulling the envelope from his pocket. 'Then take a look at these photographs.'

Bill took the photographs and quickly looked through them. He needed only a brief glance. 'Yes, that's him! That's the chap all right. But how on earth did you get these photographs?'

'Don't worry about the photographs, Bill.' Temple put out his hand for the photographs and put them back in the envelope. 'Just tell me what happened.'

'Well, they had a row, a first-class one. So far as I could tell they appeared to be arguing about a coat and the Pier at Brighton.'

'The Pier at Brighton?' said Temple, puzzled. Then suddenly, 'They must have meant the Pier Hotel.'

Mrs Fletcher had been holding a coat, Bill remembered, and was obviously trying to get Langdon to take it from her. Listening to the low-voiced conversation he had been convinced that she had undertaken to deliver the coat to some person in Brighton called Margo and had decided that she was going to have nothing to do with it, the job could be done by Julia, she said. Langdon had blustered, threatened that she would be in trouble with Dr Benkaray if she refused.

'He threatened her with Dr Benkaray?'

'Yes, Mr Temple. But Mother wasn't scared by that. She was very defiant. And she said a funny thing. She told this chap – Langdon you said his name was? – "You can say two words to Dr Benkaray, just two words. Edgar Northampton."'

'Edgar Northampton?' Temple repeated, memorising the name. 'How did Langdon react?'

'He didn't seem to know the name, but somehow Mother had the upper hand on him after that and he took the coat.'

'Do you know anyone called Northampton?'

'The only person of that name I know is the manager of the London and Southern Bank in Tenterhurst where we have our account, but I don't know his Christian name.'

A car had pulled in at the pumps. The driver was obviously a regular, for he waved at Bill and began to serve himself.

'What happened then?' Temple protested.

'The man left and I went back to bed. And I don't mind telling you I lay awake for two or three hours, trying to figure things out. And I'm no clearer about it now than I was then.'

Bill was relieved now that he had told his story and some of the strain had gone out of his face. He was watching the man operating the pump.

'Did you tell your mother what you'd heard?'

'No, I never mentioned it.'

'Did it occur to you that the Julia they were talking about was Julia Kelburn?'

'That's the girl that was murdered? No, I never thought of that.'

'She was a patient of Dr Benkaray's. So it's quite possible that your mother knew her.'

'Mr Temple, you don't think my mother had anything to do with the murder?'

'I don't think your mother committed the murder, Bill, if that's what you mean,' Temple said quickly. 'But it's my guess – she knows who did.'

'Oh, no!' Bill breathed, his distress obvious. 'If my mother's got into trouble, Mr Temple, it's because of me. She always wanted me to have a good start in life – to have a garage of my own. Even when I was a kid she . . .'

'Don't worry, Bill,' Temple reassured him. 'We'll sort this out. Now tell me, you're quite sure you heard the name Margo mentioned?'

The man at the pump had filled his tank and was replacing the filler cap. Bill was torn between going out to take his money and finishing his conversation.

'Yes, I'm positive. You believe me, don't you, Mr Temple?' Bill, his hand on the door, looked back appealingly at Temple.

'Yes, I believe you. Now listen, Bill.' Temple moved after Bill as the door opened and the bell pinged. 'Try not to worry too much about this, but keep your eyes and ears open. I'll be in touch with you.'

Temple found Steve sitting in the Rover, still staring dutifully at the blank wall ahead.

'Well!' she said, as he opened the door on the driver's side. 'I thought you'd walked out of my life.'

'Sorry, darling. I got caught up.'

Steve had not even looked round at him. 'Is it all right for me to turn my head now? My neck's frozen solid.'

'Oh, Steve! Dr Benkaray and Cross drove away a quarter of an hour ago!'

Steve made a great play of relaxing her shoulders and seeing if she could still swivel her head on her neck. 'Well, I wish someone had told me – you look very thoughtful, Paul. Has something happened?'

'I've had quite a talk with young Fletcher.' Temple reversed away from the wall, then spun the wheel to drive across the forecourt on to the road. Bill Fletcher, counting the notes his customer had handed him, gave a wave. 'That lad's an innocent, hard-working young man, but I'm afraid his mother's kept him in the dark about a lot of things. That's what's worrying him at the moment.'

Steve fastened her seat belt as Temple waited for a gap in the line of cars streaming through Westerton towards the coastal towns.

'He told me Langdon was down here a little while ago. He tried to persuade Mrs Fletcher to take a coat to someone in Brighton – someone called Margo.'

'Margo?' Steve echoed.

'Yes, but oddly enough that doesn't interest me as much as the Brighton angle. Remember Tony Wyman told me that he met Julia Kelburn's friend Fiona at Brighton.'

'You think Margo and this Fiona Scott might be one and the same person?'

'It's possible, I suppose.'

To Steve's surprise, Temple pulled and turned not towards The Red Hart but towards the town of Tenterhurst.

'Paul! Aren't you going the wrong way? The pub's at the other end of the village.'

'We'll skip The Red Hart, darling. I want to go down to Brighton.'

Steve, accustomed to Paul's sudden changes of plan, took the announcement calmly.

'Have you any idea how long we'll stay there?'

'Oh, two or three days, probably.'

'But we haven't brought any things with us. What are we going to do?'

'We'll stop in Tenterhurst and telephone Charlie. And I want to cash a cheque. We should just make it if we hurry.'

Steve glanced at her watch. It was already twenty past three.

Temple, keeping an eye on his mirrors, used the full power of the 3.5 litre engine to cover the five miles in as many minutes. It was three twenty-seven when he pulled up opposite the London and Southern Bank in the main street of Tenterhurst.

'Steve, there's a telephone kiosk across the road. You telephone Charlie while I go in to the bank.'

'Where shall I tell him we're staying?'

'What's that hotel on the front we liked the look of last year? The Pier, isn't it?'

'Yes. The Pier. Paul, you realise you're parked on a double yellow line?'

'That's just too bad, isn't it?'

Temple had seen one of the clerks at the bank's door, one half of which was closed already. He was glancing at his watch, preparatory to closing the other half on the dot of three thirty. Temple gave him a smile as he squeezed past.

The young clerk behind the first window thought he had finished business for the day and was counting his cash. He wiped the frown of annoyance from his face when he looked up and saw Temple's authoritative face.

'Good afternoon, sir.'

'Good afternoon. I'd like to cash a cheque, please.'

'Certainly, sir. You have a bank card?'

'I have, but I'm going to need more than fifty pounds.'

'How much were you wanting, sir?' the clerk said doubtfully.

'Five hundred.'

'Well, I don't know – I think you'd better speak to the manager, sir.'

'With pleasure,' Temple said, smiling.

'What is the name, please?'

'Temple. Paul Temple.'

The front door had been closed and the last of the customers were being let out one by one. Temple did not have to wait long before a door at the end of the bank opened and a middle-aged man wearing steel-rimmed spectacles came half out. He was stout and chubby-cheeked and no more than five foot four in height.

'Would you care to come into my office, Mr Temple?'

'Certainly.'

As he went towards the manager's door, Temple heard some customer who had arrived late banging angrily on the outer door. As one of the customers was let out he heard the clerk protesting that it was already past closing time. Then the manager closed the door behind him and the sound of the altercation was cut off.

At the manager's bidding Temple took the chair opposite his desk. The manager sat down in his own chair and placed his folded arms on the blotter. Like many men of small stature he became more confident when ensconced behind a desk.

'Now, I understand you'd like us to cash a cheque for five hundred pounds. You understand I shall need to telephone your own bank for clearance, and will have to charge you for the call. You have your cheque book with you?'

'Of course. I understand.' Temple was reaching into his pocket for his cheque book. 'I'm sorry to be such a nuisance, Mr—It's Mr Northampton, isn't it?'

'That's right.'

Temple took the plunge. 'Edgar Northampton?'

The manager smiled, pleased that his name was known to such a distinguished person. His work as chairman of the local committee that was agitating for a by-pass had been reported in some of the national dailies and he assumed that was where Temple had seen it.

'Yes,' he said modestly. 'That is my name.'

CHAPTER V

Breakwater House

The telephone call went through smoothly and after talking to Temple's London bank Edgar Northampton was even more effusive than before. Temple, who had only asked for such a large sum in order to be sure of seeing the manager, wrote out a cheque and asked for the money in fifty-pound notes.

'I'm very much obliged to you, Mr Northampton,' he said, when a clerk had brought ten crisp new notes in from the main bank and he had stowed them away in an inside pocket.

'Not at all, Mr Temple. Glad to be of help. Do you come down here often?'

'We sometimes stay at The Red Hart.'

'Oh, yes. The landlord is a customer of mine. Most of the Westerton business people have their accounts here.'

'Then perhaps you know Mrs Fletcher and her son. They keep the garage and filling station there.'

'Fletcher? Let me think now . . . A tall, fair-haired woman?'

'No, she's just average height, turning grey.'

'Ah, yes! I remember. We met at a garden fete about eight months ago. When she discovered I was a bank manager she was rather anxious to get my advice. Yes, of course, I remember the lady. How stupid of me!'

'I expect people are always after free advice, Mr Northampton?'

'Yes, they are.' The manager stood up. 'Still, advice costs nothing, as they say.'

As Temple left the office there was only one customer left in the main hall. He had his back turned as he stuffed the money he had collected into a small leather wallet with a wrist strap. Temple guessed that he was the customer who had so insistently demanded entry just as the bank was closing, but he did not pay him much attention. He was approaching the door, where the same clerk was waiting to let him out, when he heard his name called.

'Hello, Mr Temple. So we meet again.'

He turned round, recognising the voice as that of Larry Cross. The man had the look of someone who has managed to beat the system and secure special treatment for himself.

'Good afternoon, Mr Cross,' Temple said, polite but cool.

'They gave you the VIP treatment, I see – big welcome in the manager's office. Now I wonder what that means?' Cross managed to put both resentment and sarcasm into his question. Temple turned the insinuation aside with a laugh.

'It could mean that I have a large overdraft.'

In spite of himself Cross smiled. 'You're right there.'

'I expect you find that Alfa Romeo of yours expensive to run.'

'Alfa Romeo?' Cross echoed, swinging the wallet like a pendulum on its strap.

'The red job I saw you in the other night with Laura Kelburn.'

Cross's face was blank. 'Who's Laura Kelburn?'

'She's George Kelburn's wife. Julia's stepmother.'

'You saw me with Mrs Kelburn? Where?'

'In Leicester Square.'

Cross laughed unpleasantly. 'You certainly didn't. I don't know Mrs Kelburn. I don't know any of the Kelburns.'

'Didn't you know Julia – the dead girl?'

'No, why should I?' Cross demanded, with a touch of truculence.

'She was a patient of Dr Benkaray's.'

'So what?'

'You're the doctor's secretary. Surely you know her patients?'

'Not all of them.'

'I see,' Temple said, with hardly concealed disbelief.

A clerk had come out through a door that led through to the area behind the counter. 'You left your cheque book behind, sir.'

Cross took the book and muttered perfunctory thanks. The interruption gave him the cue he needed to escape from Temple's bland interrogation.

'Goodbye, Temple,' he flung over his shoulder before he dived out through the half-open street door. 'And if you see me in that sports car again, stop me. I'd like to take a look at it!'

'I'll bear that in mind, Mr Cross.'

Temple was usually lucky in finding parking places and as he drove up to The Pier Hotel on the front at Brighton a car reversed away from one of the four-hour parking meters outside it.

'Why are we stopping here, Paul?' Steve asked, as he slid the Rover into the vacated space. 'We usually stay at Hove.'

'This time we're staying at The Pier,' he told her and she knew from his tone of voice that it was no good questioning him further. He had been reticent about his reasons for coming down to Brighton and when she had asked if it was to look for Fiona Scott he had answered: 'Yes – amongst other things.'

The receptionist was wary as she saw two prospective guests walk in without any luggage, but she changed her attitude when she heard Temple's voice and had a closer look at Steve. Yes, it so happened that a room with bathroom was available, an 'Executive Double' facing the sea. Temple filled in the requisite form and received in reply a card with the room number written on it.

'Your room is number 288, Mr Temple. I'll call the porter to take your baggage up.'

'I'm afraid we haven't any at the moment.'

'Oh.' The receptionist looked disappointed, as if her judgement of character had been found lacking. 'In that case, sir, I'm afraid we must ask you to pay in—'

'My man's bringing our things down by train from London,' Temple reassured her. 'Would you send him up to our room as soon as he arrives?'

'Yes, of course, Mr Temple.' The girl smiled, relieved. 'Don't forget your key.'

Steve, doing a little exploration in the background, had discovered a lounge where tea was being served and as it was the hour for the ritual that was sacred in the Temple household she steered Paul in there before going up to their room. Charlie was coming down on the 16.02 train and so could not be expected for another three-quarters of an hour.

Temple chose a chair from which he could see the people moving to and from the reception desk and as Steve harked back to the unpleasant shock she had received seeing Larry Cross at Westerton – it had brought back the suffocating memory of that pad being pushed over her face at Heathrow – she was not at all sure that he was even listening to her.

Fortunately, she had finished her second cup of tea when he suddenly stood up and said: 'Come on, Steve.' He was well ahead of her as he strode out into the entrance lobby just as a man in a check jacket and fawn trousers with a raincoat over his arm finished his conversation with the receptionist. As he turned away from the counter he almost bumped into Temple.

'Oh, I beg your –' Temple began, then broke into a surprised smile. 'Well, hello, Langdon. This is a surprise!'

'Temple! Well, what do you know?' He took Temple's hand and pumped it warmly, then turned and saw Steve. His raincoat fell to the ground as he grabbed his hat off. 'Hello, Mrs Temple! Good to see you again!'

'Good afternoon, Mr Langdon.' Steve smiled as she rescued her hand from the American's warm clasp and flexed her fingers.

'Well, this really is a pleasure,' Langdon enthused. 'I'd no idea you'd be down here.'

'We felt we needed a breath of sea air,' Temple said, avoiding Steve's eye.

'You're not the only ones,' Langdon said, picking his raincoat off the floor. 'Kelburn's got the same idea. That's why I'm here. He has a suite on the first floor.'

Steve said: 'I thought you were going back to the States, Mr Langdon?'

'I was, Mrs Temple. I was due to leave this morning but Kelburn made me cancel. I guess he's got too accustomed to having me around, that's about it.'

'I'm sure you've been a great help, Langdon.'

'Yeah, I know, but he expects me to interfere in affairs which don't really concern me. He keeps asking my advice about – well, about his wife for one thing. They seem to have drifted apart these last few weeks.' Langdon lowered his voice.

'I wouldn't be surprised if they didn't split up. Only the other day Kelburn was asking my advice about getting a divorce.'

'Don't tell me he'll expect you to handle that for him!'

Langdon laughed. 'You'd be surprised what he expects me to handle, Mrs Temple.'

'Maybe he's interested in some other woman,' Temple suggested.

'Gee, no! The boot's on the other foot, if anything.' Langdon glanced round to make sure the receptionist was not listening, but he need not have worried. The girl was answering the telephone. 'I've seen Laura out twice recently with another man.'

'A tall, dark-haired hatchet-faced man of about forty?'

'Yes—could be.'

'I think you'll find he is Dr Benkaray's secretary,' Temple told him. 'That's the doctor Julia consulted.'

Langdon digested this piece of information, his expression puzzled. 'D'you know this character, then?'

'I've met him during the course of my investigations. But how did Mrs Kelburn become involved with him? That's what I'd like to know.'

'Maybe she went with Julia one day – to the doctor's, I mean . . .' Langdon broke off as the receptionist put the telephone down and came to the counter.

'Excuse me, sir. Mr Kelburn says you may go up now. It's Suite 119 – first floor.'

'Will you be staying on in London, Langdon?' Temple asked, as Langdon started towards the lift.

'That's up to Kelburn. But I can tell you this, the moment he gives the word I shall be heading back to New York.'

'Paul, how did you know?' Steve asked as soon as the couple were in the privacy of their own room.

'Know what?' Temple replied innocently.

'That George Kelburn was here and that we were going to meet Langdon. That's who you were looking out for when we were having tea, wasn't it?'

'I was hoping to see someone, but I was not sure who. I backed a hunch based on something Bill Fletcher said and it paid off.'

Their room on the second floor looked out over the promenade and the beach. On either side the two piers prodded fingers out into a sparkling sea. Steve opened the window and breathed in the tangy air. Behind her Temple was leafing through the pages of the local telephone directory.

'Langdon tried to persuade Mrs Fletcher to bring a coat down to Brighton and deliver it to Margo,' he explained.

'Do you think Margo and this girl Fiona Scott are the same person?'

'You asked me that before, Steve,' Temple reminded her, laughing. 'According to Kelburn she's a highly respectable young lady who disapproved of Julia's more sensational friends.' He threw the telephone directory on to a chair. 'All the same, she's not in the 'phone book. That would have been expecting too much.'

The wind was fresh enough to blow the curtains into the room. Steve closed the window and checked her watch.

'I wonder what time Charlie will get here. Isn't it strange to be in a hotel bedroom without any luggage?'

She was moving towards him with arms outstretched when the telephone started to ring.

'Damn!' Steve said, glaring at the instrument with dislike. 'Do you have to answer it?'

But Temple had already reached the telephone and was picking it up.

'Is that you, Temple?'

Even from the other side of the room Steve recognised the distinctive accent on the other end of the line. Sir Graham Forbes's voice was so strong that she was able to hear every word of the ensuing conversation.

'Hello, Sir Graham! Are you speaking from London?'

'Yes.'

'How did you know we were down here?'

'Charlie told me. What are you doing in Brighton anyway?'

'Oh – we just thought we'd pop down here for a breath of sea air.' Temple smiled at Steve.

'I see.' Forbes paused before playing the card he had up his sleeve. 'I thought perhaps you might be looking for a girl named Fiona Scott.'

'How did you find out the name?' Temple asked with some surprise.

'What's more to the point – how did you find it?'

'I had a talk with Tony Wyman. He apparently met her some little time ago.'

'I see. Well, listen, Temple – we've got her 'phone number. Have you a pen?'

Temple pulled out a pen and signalled Steve to bring him something to write on. She ran to the writing-table and picked up a sheet of the hotel's notepaper. Temple nodded his thanks as he wrote the number down.

'We haven't contacted her yet because we don't want to scare the girl,' Forbes went on. 'I thought you might 'phone her – unofficially, as it were – and get the lie of the land.'

'Yes, all right, Sir Graham,' Temple agreed with some amusement. 'How did you get the number?'

'We do find things out for ourselves occasionally,' Forbes said drily. 'Keep in touch, Temple. Love to Steve.'

Temple was still laughing when he put the 'phone down.

'What's the joke?' Steve enquired.

'That was Sir Graham, as I expect you guessed. Charlie told him we were down here. He's given me Fiona Scott's 'phone number.'

'I'll bet Raine found it. He'd make sure you weren't going to put one over on him.' Steve had adopted an expression which Temple knew well. It meant that she had her thinking cap on. 'You know what I would do, Paul, if I were investigating this case?'

'What *would* you do, darling?'

'I should forget all about Fiona Scott and concentrate on Mike Langdon. There's something about him—'

'And what about all the other suspects?' Temple objected, laughing. 'Larry Cross, Tony Wyman, Mrs Fletcher, Dr Benkaray – even Edgar Northampton.'

'The bank manager? You don't think he had anything to do with the murder?'

'No, I don't.' Temple had started to dial the number Forbes had given him. 'But Bill Fletcher implied that he had some sort of hold over Dr Benkaray. Hello! Could I speak to Miss Fiona Scott, please?'

The voice of the woman who answered was so low that Steve did not even try to follow the conversation. She went to the window to watch the evening traffic on the road below. People who had been at work all day had come out to stroll along the promenade. A few fresh-air fiends were striding along briskly, taking deep breaths as they put their best foot forward. Out on the water a windsurfer was struggling to right his capsized board. As always at Brighton there was plenty to entertain the interested observer.

'Well, I finally got through to Fiona Scott,' Temple said, putting the 'phone down.

'Did you get anything from her?'

'She was evasive at first; didn't want to have anything more to do with the affair of Julia. But she relented when I told her that she was probably fonder of Julia than anyone else and could almost certainly tell me a few things that would be useful.'

'Are you going to see her?'

'Apparently I only just caught her. She's going away to stay with some friends of hers who live at a place called Seadale—'

'That's further along the coast, about fifteen miles from here.'

'Yes. She said that if I drive over there this evening she would talk to me.'

'What time?'

'Eight o'clock. A place called Breakwater House, a mile or two beyond the village.'

'We'll need to have an early – Come in!'

Steve had stopped at the sound of knuckles rapping on the door. She knew it was not locked, but as there was no response she went over and opened it. The figure standing in the corridor outside had a suitcase in each hand. He was wearing a check shower-proof overcoat, which had once belonged to Temple, and a jaunty tweed hat perched incongruously on his head. 'Hello, Mrs Temple!'

'Oh, hello, Charlie.' The spectacle of Charlie in a hat was so unusual that Steve just stood there staring at him.

'You haven't wasted much time!' Temple exclaimed.

'No, wonderful train service!' As Steve stood aside Charlie proceeded into the room and put the case down in the middle of the carpet. 'Just caught the four o'clock as it was pulling out. Here's your case, Mrs Temple – and here's yours, sir.'

'Thank you, Charlie. What's that small case?'

'Oh, this.' Charlie removed the hat and wiped his brow with the back of his hand. 'I brought the recorder down, Mr Temple. I thought I'd tape the 'phone calls while you were away, so you could hear them for yourself. Better than writing a message down.'

'Much better, Charlie,' Temple agreed solemnly. 'Put it down on that table. There's a socket in the wall underneath. Have there been many calls?'

'Only two important ones. Sir Graham rang, but he only wanted to know where you were. The first call was from a woman – wouldn't give her name or anything.'

'What time was this?'

'Oh, about half past ten this morning.'

While Charlie took his overcoat off, carefully folded it and placed it on a chair near the door, with the hat on top, Temple plugged the telephone monitoring machine in. Steve sat down in the chair beside the window, waiting expectantly. Charlie, looking around for somewhere suitable to sit, decided against the bed and perched uncomfortably astride the suitcases.

Temple made sure that the tape had been wound back, switched the machine on and sat down in the chair by the table. The hum of the machine filled the room and then the brr-brr of the 'phone ringing followed by Charlie picking up the receiver.

'Mr Temple's residence,' came the voice of Charlie.

'Can I speak to Mr Temple, please?'

'I'm afraid he's away at the moment. Who is that?'

'Can you tell me where I can get in touch with him?'

'Who is that speaking?'

The woman hesitated, obviously reluctant to give her name, but Temple had already recognised the voice as Mrs Fletcher's.

'You wouldn't know my name . . . Where is Mr Temple?'

'He's gone down to Brighton for a few days with Mrs Temple.'

'Why has he gone to Brighton?' Mrs Fletcher sounded alarmed at mention of Brighton. 'Do you know?'

'No, I'm sorry, I don't know.'

'Is he – Is he going to the fun fair?'

'Don't ask me,' Charlie chuckled. 'Shouldn't think so. Not Mr Temple's cup of tea. Look – if you leave your name . . .'

'Where is Mr Temple staying?'

'I'm sorry, I don't know.'

'All right, I'll ring back later!'

As the amplified clicks and rattles started again Temple switched off the machine.

'Did you recognise the voice, Paul?'

'Yes – it was Mrs Fletcher.'

'Made me laugh when she mentioned the fun fair . . .' Charlie was chuckling again as he remembered Mrs Fletcher's improbable question. Steve too was smiling at the idea. 'I can't imagine you and Mr Temple on the dodgems.'

Charlie was trying to bring Temple in on the joke, but Temple's face was serious.

'Can't you, Charlie?' he said thoughtfully. 'All right, let's hear the next one.'

The second conversation was both shorter and more to the point. The caller was Laura Kelburn and when she heard that the Temples were away she had no hesitation in asking Charlie to give Temple a message. 'Mr Temple saw me in a friend's car the other night near Hyde Park Corner. I'm very anxious that he shouldn't mention the fact to anyone – particularly my husband.'

Temple switched the machine off and unplugged it. 'Well done, Charlie. It's a great help to hear people's tone of voice. You can take this back to London with you.'

'Well,' Steve said, 'that ties up with what Mike Langdon said, doesn't it, Paul?'

'You mean another man and the possibility of Kelburn getting a divorce? I find it hard to believe Laura Kelburn's fallen for someone like Larry Cross.'

'You never can tell,' Steve reminded him with a smile. 'Women are peculiar creatures.'

'You can say that . . .' Charlie began with feeling, then clapped his hand over his mouth. 'Oh, I beg your pardon, Mrs Temple.'

Charlie had stood up in his confusion. Temple kept a straight face.

'You'd better get back to town, Charlie. Are you all right for money?'

'Yes – fine.' Charlie had taken the hint and was closing the case containing the recorder. 'All right if I take a taxi back to the station? I can just catch the 5.59.'

'Yes, take a taxi and keep taping the 'phone calls. You know where we are if there's anything urgent.'

'Yes, sir! Goodbye, Mrs Temple.' Charlie gathered up his hat and coat and put a hand on the door. 'Don't eat too much rock.'

'Goodbye, Charlie,' Temple said, in a tone of firm dismissal, but when the door had closed on Charlie he burst out laughing.

'Paul, why do you think Mrs Fletcher mentioned the fun fair?'

'I don't know. But she obviously thought that was one of the reasons why we came here.'

Temple picked up the suitcases and put them one on each side of the bed, where they would be easy to unpack.

'But why on earth should she think that?'

'We won't know until we visit the place.'

'I can't wait for that!' Steve said, snapping the catches on her case.

'Even then it might not be clear what she was getting at. You see, if there's someone there that she doesn't want us to . . .'

Temple broke off as a knock sounded on the door. They stared at each other with exasperation.

'Charlie's forgotten something!' Temple murmured. Then he called, more loudly: 'Come in!'

It was not Charlie who walked into the room but George Kelburn. He closed it behind him before asking, 'Can you spare me a minute, Temple?'

For his visit to Brighton, Kelburn had selected a brown blazer with plain brass buttons and a pair of sponge-bag check trousers. In his holiday gear he seemed less formidable than in his business suit and this impression was reinforced by an unwontedly apologetic manner.

'Yes, of course – come on in, Kelburn. You know my wife?'

'Yes, I do.' Kelburn inclined his head towards Steve. 'Good afternoon, Mrs Temple.'

'Good afternoon, Mr Kelburn. Do sit down.'

The invitation was automatic. In fact the provision of chairs was sparse and she was relieved when he shook his head.

'I'd rather stand, if you don't mind. I'm very restless today, for some reason or other.' Kelburn illustrated his point by crossing the room and standing in front of the electric fire, the nearest he could get to his favourite position in front of the mantelpiece. 'Mrs Temple, I'd like to apologise for my rudeness the last time we met. I have rather an abrupt manner at times and it occasionally – well – gives the wrong impression.'

'That's all right, Mr Kelburn,' Steve said, responding to his shamefaced smile.

'The same applies to our last meeting, Temple. You were perfectly right, of course – no reason why you shouldn't continue your investigations if you feel like it. Quite understandable to want to keep on with a case once you've started it.' He paused, and then asked casually: 'Incidentally, is that why you're down here in Brighton?'

'No,' Temple replied, just as casually. 'My wife had a rather unpleasant experience just lately; we thought a change of air might do her good.'

'Yes, of course.' Kelburn nodded emphatically, accepting the explanation. 'Well, I'll tell you what I wanted to have a word with you about, Temple. It's rather a delicate matter. You'll treat this in the strictest confidence?'

'Yes, of course.'

Still restless, Kelburn moved to the window and glanced down at the street, almost as if he expected to see some covert watcher. Steve now had access to the one armchair and promptly sat down in it.

'Well, I don't know whether Langdon mentioned this to you or not but . . .' He hesitated and then blurted out: 'I'm afraid I'm having trouble with my wife.'

'What kind of trouble?' Temple asked.

'She stays out late, doesn't tell me where she's been, and – well – to be perfectly honest, I think she's having an affair with someone.'

'Have you any idea who it is?'

'No, I haven't.'

'Have you spoken to her about it, Mr Kelburn?'

'Yes, but she refuses to admit that there is anyone. But there is someone – I'm sure there is. Of course, she has a

123

large circle of friends and according to Langdon she's been seeing a lot of Tony Wyman lately, but whether he's the man or not I wouldn't know.'

'Well, what do you want me to do?' Except to turn and face Kelburn in his changes of position, Temple had not moved from his position at the foot of the bed.

'I'd like you to make some enquiries for me, watch her, if possible.' He added quickly, as he saw Temple frown: 'Oh, I know this isn't your usual line of country . . .'

Temple laughed. 'It certainly isn't!'

'But if I employed one of the usual agencies Laura would be on to it straight away, I'm sure she would.'

'And you don't think she'd suspect me?'

'No, I'm positive she wouldn't. She might even confide in you. I'm convinced you're the man for this assignment, Temple.'

Temple met his eye thoughtfully and Kelburn made a point of not dropping his own direct gaze – reminiscent of some senior officer assigning a subaltern to a dangerous mission. 'Does Mike Langdon agree with you?'

Kelburn was surprised by the question. 'Yes, he does.'

'Well, I'll think about it.'

Kelburn was not accustomed to waiting for other people's decisions. With a return to his customary brusque manner he said: 'All right – but don't think about it too long. It's important.' He was already crossing from the window to the door. 'I won't mention a fee because the last time I mentioned money . . .'

'I'll let you have a decision this evening. You'll be in the hotel, I take it?'

'Yes, I will. I'm dining here. Thank you, Temple.' As he opened the door Kelburn remembered his manners. He gave Steve the same brief nod as when he had come in. 'Goodbye, Mrs Temple.'

'Paul, do you know what I think . . .' Steve got up from her chair as soon as the door had closed.

'No, darling, what do you think?'

'I don't think Kelburn's worried about his wife. I think this is just an attempt to stop you investigating the murder.'

Steve was opening the window. Kelburn had been wearing some kind of aftershave or deodorant and it hung in the room. She felt that a gust of sea air would purify the atmosphere. Temple had opened his suitcase and found a cardigan thoughtfully packed by Charlie.

'On the other hand, Laura is friendly with someone, remember. That's why she telephoned me, because she didn't want us to tell her husband about seeing her with Larry Cross.'

'Yes, but I still don't think that's why he consulted you. For some reason or other Kelburn wants you to drop this case. If he can't get you to drop it, then he'll try and divert your attention on to something else.'

Temple had removed his jacket to put on the cardigan. 'Meaning his wife?'

'Yes.'

'M'm, could be. Well, come along, Steve. You'd better bring a woolly.'

'Where are we going?'

'Do you feel like a nice smooth ride on a roller-coaster?'

'Paul, my head's splitting. Can't we go back to the hotel? If we're going to be in time for—'

'Just a bit longer, Steve. We haven't seen that part over there, behind the shooting gallery.'

It was a real old-fashioned fair with panting steam engines, merry-go-rounds, dodgems, hobby-horses, whirling swings, shooting galleries and every kind of side-show from the Fat Lady to the Troupe of Performing Fleas. The din was deafening, what with the blaring music, the crack of shots, the shouts of the touts and the screams of children. To Steve's intense relief there was no roller-coaster but the giant wheel had given her a bad attack of vertigo.

'But the shooting gallery is where we came in!' Steve protested, her head spinning.

'No, dear,' Paul told her patiently. 'That was on the other side, near the ghost train—'

'Don't mention that ghost train!' she protested, wincing at the memory of those clammy, cold hands brushing her face and hair.

Holding Temple's hand and stumbling through the crowd behind him, she let herself be towed round the side of the shooting gallery.

'Paul, I'm being deafened by those guns.'

'Shan't be much longer, darling. I just want to make sure – By Timothy!'

'What is it?'

'Look at that sign, on the tent over by the coconut-shy.'

Focussing her eyes with an effort she peered through the smoky haze. Though it was not yet dark the fairground lights had been switched on and she could see the name on a board over the opening of the tent.

MADAME MARGO. FORTUNE TELLER.

'So that's what Mrs Fletcher meant. She thought you'd found out about Margo and that was the reason you'd come down to Brighton.'

'You may be right, Steve. Now listen – I want you to go in and have your fortune told. I'll tell you exactly what to do . . .'

126

*

Steve had to stoop to enter the tent. The interior was cramped and there was barely room for two chairs on either side of a small table, one with arms and one without. A lamp with a low-watt bulb and a thick scarlet tasselled shade cast a dim light on the table and the imitation round Persian carpet beneath it. The striped tent, luminous with the light from the fairground outside, created an eerie effect. The plump woman in gypsy costume seated in the armchair was sipping a cup of tea she had made on a calor gas stove beside her chair. In the dim light Steve could hardly see her features, but a pair of observant eyes shone in the light reflected upwards from the table.

'I'm so sorry, madam – do come in.' Madame Margo put the cup down on the floor beside her. Her accent was broad Cockney. 'I was just 'avin' a cup of tea.'

'I can wait.'

'No, no . . .' Madame Margo waved a pudgy hand at the upright chair. 'Please sit down, madam.'

Steve sat down facing the fortune teller and folded her hands on the baize-covered table. 'You are Madame Margo?'

'That's right, dear. They all know me in Brighton. Been here for years . . . Patronised by royalty . . .'

'Royalty?'

The way the lamp was angled it shone on the face of the sitter and left Madame Margo in the shade.

'His Royal Highness, Prince Castrola of Tian See. Nice young man, he was, but you never saw anything like his lifeline . . . Now what sort of reading did you want?'

'I don't know. Which would you recommend?'

127

'Looking at you, I'd say the palm, madam. Of course, it's a bit more expensive, but it goes deeper – much deeper, if you know what I mean.'

As Steve's eyes accustomed themselves, the face of the fortune teller was becoming clearer. The features above the bizarre gypsy costume were plump and at the same time avaricious.

'Yes, you read the palm of a friend of mine and told her the most amazing story – it all came true. That's what made me so curious.'

'Did I? I wonder if I remember her?'

'I'm sure you would. You foretold a great tragedy in her life. And it happened, just as you said.'

'Really? Of course, there's no getting away from the palm. It's all there. What happened to your friend?'

'She was murdered.'

Madame Margo leant back in her chair, further from the circle of light. 'Murdered?'

'Yes. Her name was Julia Kelburn.'

'Oh, yes,' Madame Margo said, after a brief pause. 'I think I read about the murder.'

'But you don't remember Julia?'

'No, I'm afraid I don't. But, of course, I see so many people, you know, especially in the height of the season.'

'Yes, I suppose you do.'

'Now, dear, if you'll just sit facing me . . .' If she had been taken aback the older woman had recovered her poise and her professional manner. She leant forward again.

'Which hand do you want?'

'Oh, both, dear . . . Under the light if you don't mind. That's it . . .'

Steve placed her hands, palms upward, on the table. They

seemed strangely remote under the light, as if they did not belong to her. The fortune teller stared at them, gently tracing the lines with the tip of her index finger. The contact sent a tremor up Steve's arm.

'That's very interesting . . . Were you ever on the stage?'

'No,' Steve admitted. 'I wasn't.'

'You're married, and your husband's, well known – famous, in fact . . . Got something to do with books and writing, is that right, dear . . . ?'

'Yes.'

'It's an interesting hand. You travel a lot, don't you – er – Mrs . . . ?'

Steve glanced up and met the sharp eyes which were now on her face and not her hands. She ignored the invitation to give her name.

'Yes, we travel quite a lot.'

Madame Margo bent over her hand again. 'I can see a journey now . . . towards the end of the year . . . a sea voyage . . .' Suddenly the fortune teller caught her breath. 'Oh! . . . There's danger too, dear. You've got to be very careful – both you and your husband.'

There was a note of genuine warning in her voice, which Steve found convincing.

'Why have we got to be careful?'

'Because I can see an accident.' Madame Margo was gazing deeply into Steve's left palm. 'A car accident . . .'

'When is this accident likely to happen?' Steve asked, shaken by the woman's urgent tone.

'I can't tell you. It may be soon . . . very soon.' The voice was different, like that of a person talking in their sleep.

'Where is it going to happen?'

'I don't know, but . . .'

Steve's left palm was prickling under that intense scrutiny, even though Madame Margo had only her eyes on it. 'Go on . . .' she whispered.

'It seems to me your husband's driving . . . There's something here, in your palm . . . I can't tell what it is . . . It looks like a dolphin.'

'A dolphin? You mean a real dolphin?'

'I can't tell . . . But watch out for it . . .' The strange sensation went out of Steve's palm and when she looked up she found the small dark eyes staring at her. Madame Margo's voice had reverted to its normal Cockney friendliness. 'When you see the dolphin be on your guard, dear. That's when the accident might happen.'

Steve panicked for a moment when she came out of the tent and saw no sign of Temple. Then, to her relief, she spotted him over by the coconut-shy. He was just collecting a teddy-bear, his prize for knocking down the maximum number of coconuts. He was surprised at the eagerness with which she clutched his arm and hung on to it until they had passed through the exit from the fairground. Only when they were away from the merry but oppressive din did she try to give him a description of her experience in Madame Margo's tent.

'It was only when I mentioned Julia Kelburn that she seemed to be on her guard,' she finished. 'I think she had a good idea who I was.'

'Yes, it sounds like it. D'you think she was expecting you?'

'I don't know. The whole set-up was terribly phoney and normally I wouldn't believe a word she said, but that was a warning, Paul, about the car accident – I don't think there's any doubt about that.'

'That's why I asked if you thought she was expecting you. This way, Steve. The car's over here.'

'It's difficult to say. But the thing that puzzled me is that reference to a dolphin. What did she mean – watch out for the dolphin?'

'I don't know. It could be a public house, I suppose, at a dangerous corner or crossroads.'

'Yes, I wonder why I never thought of that.'

Temple opened the car door for Steve before going round to his own side. As he slid into the driver's seat he saw her press her fingers to her eyes.

'Tired?'

'Yes, I am. It was a draining experience.'

'Well, there's no need for you to come to Seadale, darling. I can see Fiona Scott by myself.'

'Yes, of course you can,' Steve agreed. She waited while Temple operated the self-starter and then straightened her shoulders. 'But you're not going to.'

'This has got to be the road. Fiona Scott said you couldn't miss it if you kept as close to the sea as possible.'

They had taken a right turn after passing through the hamlet of Seadale, but the road had soon deteriorated into a lane and after a mile or so had swung inland away from the coast. The headlights of the Rover illuminated rough banks hemming the lane in and beyond them scraggy trees twisted into tormented shapes by the inshore winds. They had not passed a house since leaving the main road and fortunately had met no other cars. That would have meant reversing to one of the occasional passing places.

'If we don't come to something soon, I'm going to turn round,' Temple said. 'We must have missed a turning.'

As they rounded yet another bend, Steve exclaimed: 'Look, Paul, there's a light ahead.'

It was a wavering light and almost gave the impression that someone was signalling. After a hundred yards Temple dipped his headlights.

'I think it's a cyclist. We must have nearly blinded him.'

In fact, the cyclist had dismounted and was waiting for them to pass. As they drew near Temple saw the white collar and the dark grey suit of a clergyman. He was wearing a battered brown felt hat and had his head lowered to avoid the glare of the headlamps. As Temple drew up beside him he raised his head. He was about fifty and had the craggy but charitable features of a Rugby player turned parish priest.

'Good evening,' Temple said. 'I wonder if you could help me. We're looking for a place called Breakwater House.'

'Ah, yes . . . Breakwater House.' The vicar peered into the car, trying to see how many passengers there were, but Temple's voice had reassured him. 'Now let me see . . . It's a little off the beaten track. Yes, I think it would be a better idea if you turned round . . .'

'You mean, go back?'

'That's right. You must keep a careful look out for a turning on the left – rather a narrow track.'

'Can you give me any idea how far back it is?'

'I should say nearly a mile.' The vicar used his free hand to illustrate his instructions. 'It's just past a large, old-fashioned barn.'

'Yes, I remember passing it now. Breakwater House is actually down that track?'

'Yes, indeed. The gates are about a quarter of a mile—'

'Do you know the people who live there?'

'No. It's outside my parish. But I do know there's rather a delightful arch at the entrance to the drive, with a stone dolphin on top.'

'A dolphin?' Steve stared at the clergyman. 'Did you say a dolphin?'

The vicar stooped, trying to see her face. 'Yes. Do look out for it, a beautiful piece of work, although I suppose it's rather on the dark side tonight, unfortunately.'

'I'm much obliged,' said Temple.

'Not at all, not at all. I'm sure you won't have any trouble finding it.' The vicar started to push his bike past the Rover. 'Good night.'

'Good night,' Temple called after him, 'and thank you.'

They had to go on half a mile before Temple found a place to turn the car. He had to reverse several times and he did not want to ask Steve to get out to guide him. She had been very silent since the parson had mentioned the dolphin.

As they bumped back down the lane she said: 'Paul, you heard what he—'

'Yes, I heard. Don't worry, darling, I'll take care.'

They came to the barn and the narrow track on the left without catching up with the vicar, whose bike was as fast as a car on this surface. The barn was thatched but the straw had rotted and was sagging in several places. Temple was reassured when he saw tyre marks on the track, but it was so narrow that the brambles in the hedge clawed at the car. The vicar's quarter of a mile seemed much longer but at last the headlights picked up a massive stone gateway surrounded by an arch. Its pallid shape loomed up incongruously in the lights. Heavy wrought-iron gates stood open and beyond them stretched the black tunnel of a tree-lined avenue.

Temple stopped short of the gates and felt in the glove pocket for the torch. Lowering the window he leaned out and directed the beam at the archway. Placed centrally at the top was a large and beautifully carved stone dolphin, a shark-like fin protruding from its back.

Steve shivered. 'Close the window, Paul. I'm cold.'

Temple extinguished the torch and closed the window. In bottom gear he eased through the gateway. Ahead the trees stretched upwards into darkness like the columns of a cathedral.

'Slowly, Paul,' Steve cautioned nervously.

'I can't go much slower than this, darling.'

The car was lurching and wallowing on the appalling surface and Temple was beginning to wonder what possessed Fiona Scott's friends to live in such a God-forsaken place – if indeed they did live here. Suddenly he slammed the brakes on. The wheels locked and the car slid forward a few yards, slewing sideways.

'Paul, what is it?'

'Look.'

Temple nodded at the darkness ahead. At first Steve could see nothing. Then she thought her eyes were deceiving her for a shimmering strand of light was poised in the air just in front of the car.

'What is it?'

'Looks like wire. Lucky we did not hit it at speed or—'

Temple climbed out of the car, taking the torch with him. She saw him inspect the two stout trees standing like sentinels on either side of the avenue. The gathering darkness, the silent wood, the surreptitious calls of night birds reminded her of that other evening when they had come upon the dying Ted Angus.

When Temple came back he was shaking his head. 'It's no good. You'd need wire cutters. Someone's made a good job of it.'

'What are we going to do?'

'Well,' Temple said unhappily, 'we can't take the car any further, so I suppose the only thing to do is turn back.'

She heard the disappointment in his voice and made an effort to overcome her apprehension. 'Unless – we walk. That's what you'd like to do, isn't it?'

'Yes, but if you're worried, Steve—'

'No, I'm all right.' Steve opened her door. 'Let's see if we can find the house.'

Temple turned the lights off and withdrew the ignition key, but in such an isolated spot there seemed no point in locking the doors.

'Are you sure you feel like doing this?' he said, as he joined Steve.

'Yes, I'm sure. Give me your arm, darling.'

They had gone a hundred yards further up the dark avenue, using the jagged strip of pale sky above them as a guide, when Steve said: 'If I'd known we were coming on a ramble I'd have worn some sensible shoes.'

'I didn't know you had any.'

She shook his arm. 'You know perfectly well what I mean.' They both laughed and then Steve stopped and froze. 'Paul, listen! What's that noise?'

From somewhere ahead came a low regular swishing sound, followed by a long, drawn-out rattle, rather as if some monstrous animal was writhing in its death-throes.

'It's the sea,' Paul said, after a moment. 'We must be quite near it.'

'Of course.' Steve breathed again. 'That must be why it's called Breakwater House.'

Temple was saving his torch battery and they came on the house unexpectedly. All of a sudden it was there in front of them, its blank unlit windows staring at them from twenty yards away. Steve was holding tight to Temple's arm as he shone the beam through the ground-floor windows. The place was derelict, no furniture, no carpets, paper peeling from the walls.

'There's no one living here.'

'But Paul, that fortune teller must have known we were coming here and what's more that someone was going to try and stop us.'

'Which is a very good reason for finding out what's here. I wonder if there's another way in.'

The massive front door was immovable and so was a back door leading to what had been the servants' quarters, but at the side of the house facing the sea was a set of french windows opening on to a moss-covered terrace. Temple's torch showed that this must have been an imposing drawing-room with a fireplace in the Adam style.

'That should not be too difficult to force,' he muttered, 'if I can find some sort of lever.'

Playing the torch on the ground, he began to prowl round the edge of the terrace. Steve waited by the french windows listening to the menacing sound of the sea.

When Temple rejoined her, he was holding a yard-long metal bar which he had wrenched off an old iron fence. He inserted it between the glazed doors just above the handle and as he applied leverage the lock was torn out of the rotting wood. With Steve on his heels he stepped over the threshold, playing the torch ahead of him.

The drawing-room contained nothing of interest, nor did the other rooms on the ground floor – a dining-room, a gunroom and, to judge from the bookshelves, what must have been a library. They were standing in the hall when they both heard it, a bumping noise from somewhere upstairs.

'There's someone up there,' Steve whispered.

'Come on. Keep close to me.'

Temple was glad he had some kind of weapon as they went up the broad, creaking staircase.

'There's a funny smell, Paul.' Steve was still talking in a whisper. 'What is it?'

'Smells like paraffin. There's obviously no electricity here and I expect someone's been using oil lamps.'

They were half-way up when they heard the cry, the words muffled and hard to locate. 'Help! Help! Up here. In the bedroom.'

Temple took the remaining stairs two at a time and Steve stumbled after him, anxious to remain close to him in the dark house. She saw him enter a room the door of which gaped open. She ran after him. He was standing in the middle of the room, directing the torch beam into every corner.

'What an enormous bedroom!'

'Yes, by Timothy! It's as big as Hyde Park. That must be a dressing-room.'

He was heading for a door beside the window when Steve heard a thud behind her. She spun round and saw that the door had closed.

'Paul—'

He stopped in the doorway of the dressing-room and shone the torch in her direction. She saw her own enormous shadow grow smaller as she approached the door. She seized the handle but before she had time to twist it she heard the click of a key in the lock. When she wrenched at the door it would not budge. She stared at it, not wanting to face the torch. 'We've been locked in.'

CHAPTER VI

The Late Tony Wyman

'Did you see anything?'

'No. I just heard the thud of the door closing and then the click of the lock. Paul, has someone been watching us all the time?'

Temple did not reply. The answer to that question was obvious. He handed Steve the torch, with instructions to direct the beam at the door. He tried to force the metal bar between the door and the frame, but the crack was too narrow. He switched his attention to the side where the hinges were fixed and, sure enough, there were signs of rot in the frame on that side. Using the jagged end of the bar he began to gouge the mouldering wood out and had just made a hole big enough to insert the bar when Steve said: 'Paul! I can smell burning. And there's smoke coming under the door.'

'That smell of paraffin! I ought to have realised! Someone intended to burn the place down and we interrupted them.'

They could now hear the crackling of flames beyond the door. Temple attacked the door with renewed fury.

'What about the window? Can we get out that way?'

'Not without breaking our legs. Besides, you heard that call for help.'

Temple had at last got his bar between door and frame. As he pulled on it the hinge came loose with a splintering of wood. Crouching down he worked on the lower hinge and after a couple of minutes it too yielded. Smoke forced its way through the gap. Both of them began to cough.

'We need something to cover our faces. Those curtains will do.'

He wrenched a tattered lace curtain from one of the windows. By good fortune there was water in the cold tap of the washbasin. He tore the curtain into two strips and doused them in the basin. They tied the material over their faces as makeshift masks.

'Keep behind me, Steve,' Temple said, as he grasped the hinge end of the door. 'We'll have to crawl. The smoke won't be so thick near the floor.'

At the first tug the door came free and crashed to the floor. Immediately smoke billowed in. Temple dropped to his hands and knees, his eyes already smarting. Ahead he could see the staircase blazing. The leaping flames were so bright that he had no need of the torch. Remembering the lay-out of the upper landing he turned left and, still crawling, moved along close to the wall. He glanced round once to make sure that Steve was behind him. The acrid smoke affected their eyes so much that seeing their way was as difficult as breathing. To his great relief Temple's fingers found a door at the point where a corridor led off the landing. It was open, and as soon as Steve was through he slammed it shut. It would serve as a fire-break, isolating them temporarily from the inferno.

Already the heat and smoke were less but Steve was coughing and wiping her eyes. As he helped her to her feet they heard the muffled cries for help.

'Help! Please help me!'

'It's along this corridor somewhere,' Temple muttered. 'These look like the old servants' rooms.'

Guided by the cries, they pushed further along the corridor, using the torch again now.

'Where are you?' Temple shouted.

'Here! Is that Temple? I'm in here.'

Temple opened the second door on the left, shone the torch and stopped. Behind him Steve gasped. 'Oh, my God!'

The only piece of furniture in the room was an upright ladder-backed chair. A man had been tied to it with his arms pinioned behind it and his ankles lashed to the cross-bar so that his feet were off the floor. In his struggles he had capsized the chair so that he lay at an excruciating angle, adding to his own torment. A crude gag had been inexpertly fastened into his mouth but he had managed to force it out enough to shout through the cloth.

'Temple. Thank God you've come! Let me loose! This cord is cutting like hell.'

'It's Tony Wyman! Tony, how on earth did you get here?'

Wyman's answer was a gasp of agony. To judge from the state of his face he had suffered the same treatment as Ted Angus and there was no knowing what injuries were concealed by his clothing.

With Steve's help Temple righted the chair. As he did so Wyman screamed and his head fell downwards. The pain had made him momentarily lose consciousness. Temple removed the gag, made sure his breathing was clear and then, as Steve held the torch, set to work on the viciously tight knots. Before he had finished Wyman was groaning again.

'Temple, don't let them—'

'It's all right, Tony. We'll soon have you out of here.'

Freed from the cords Wyman was collapsing in the chair. Temple stooped and scooped him up in a fireman's lift, his right arm round the back of Wyman's knees and the man's head dangling down his back. He heard Wyman groan but there was no alternative to this summary treatment. With the door at the end of the corridor blistering with the heat, they were all three in danger of being asphyxiated.

Temple was gambling on there being a service staircase leading down to the back door. With Steve going in front to light the way he carried his burden to the end of the passage. As he had expected, a narrow flight of stairs led down to the kitchen passage, at the end of which was the back door.

The smoke was less here, but he knew from the limp feel of Wyman's body that he had passed out again. Once they had reached ground level Steve ran ahead. She drew back the two heavy bolts at the top and bottom of the door and turned the huge key. As she opened it a blast of fresh sea air blew in.

Strong as he was Temple's legs were beginning to buckle as he brought Wyman to a garden seat about a hundred yards from the house. He gently laid his burden down on it and straightened up, gasping for breath. He felt Steve's hand grip his. They stood there, gazing back at the blazing house. As they watched there was a rumble and beyond the cracked windows the glow of flames intensified. The main staircase had collapsed.

'They double-crossed me—' Behind them Wyman had recovered consciousness again. 'They said they were going to –'

'He's in a bad way, Paul. That's a very serious head wound and he may have internal injuries as well.'

'Yes. We've got to get help. I don't want to move him any more.'

'Temple—' Wyman whispered.

Temple stooped to hear what he was trying to say. The roar of the fire drowned all the sounds of the night.

'What is it, Tony?'

'I've got to tell you—'

'Go on.'

'About Kelburn—'

'Yes?'

'You know Kelburn?'

'George Kelburn. Yes. What about him?'

'Kelburn – the fence – don't let him get near – don't let him touch—'

'What do you mean, Tony? What are you trying to say?'

'He's passed out again, Paul. It's no good. He'll die if he doesn't get attention soon! You go back to the car and I'll stay with him!'

But Temple would not agree to that. He had no intention of leaving Steve beside that roaring inferno with God knows who lurking in the shadows. In any case, there was nothing she could do for Wyman.

They made him as comfortable as they could with Temple's jacket under his head and Steve's coat over him and left him with the glow of the burning house playing on his bloodied face.

The tree-lined avenue was so brightly lit by the burning house behind them that they did not need to use the torch till they had reached the first bend.

'We'll have to watch out for that wire, Steve. Better keep behind me.'

'That fire – it seemed to blaze up so quickly.'

'That was because of the paraffin. You saw how thick the smoke was.'

Steve was having difficulty in keeping up. Her high heels kept catching in the uneven surface. 'Paul, Tony Wyman didn't seem surprised that it was you. I almost felt he was expecting you to turn up. What was he doing in that house?'

'That's the biggest mystery of all. But someone obviously resented him being there and gave the poor devil a heavy beating.'

'I'm beginning to wonder if there really is such a person as Fiona Scott.'

'She was probably acting on instructions – ah, here's the wire. Go round the outside of this tree.'

The car was a haven and Steve was grateful to slip into the passenger's seat and take off her shoes. Temple climbed in beside her and switched the lights on.

'We'll go back towards Seadale and see if we can find a call-box.' He twisted the ignition key and the starter motor turned over, but there was no spark from the engine. He gave the starter a long burst of ten seconds but the engine remained dead. His face grim, he reached down to the release catch, then took the torch and got out to open the bonnet. Steve saw him bend over the engine compartment. After a few seconds he straightened up and closed the bonnet.

'Someone's taken the rotor-arm out,' he told her. 'The car's useless.'

'Are you sure?'

'I'm positive. We'll have to walk. Come on, it's not all that far to the gate.'

Wincing, Steve pushed her aching feet into her shoes again.

They were half-way to the gates when Temple heard a low humming sound to the right of the avenue. The beam of the torch was strong enough to show up a small building half hidden by rhododendrons.

'What is it, Paul?'

'Some sort of power-house. Let's take a look at it.'

'Be careful.'

As they approached, the humming noise became identifiable as a small motor. There were no windows and the low door was firmly padlocked. Temple inspected the padlock, which had been recently oiled.

'It's a power-house.'

'But what's it for?'

'Must be to supply electricity to the house.'

'But there were no lights.'

'Perhaps the main switch had been turned off.' Temple dismissed the problem for the moment. 'Come on, Steve. It's more important for us to get help for Wyman.'

The gates were only fifty yards further on. The glow of the fire was reflected earthwards by the low clouds and it shed an amber-coloured artificial moonlight on the trees and the stone archway. Not till they were quite close, however, could Steve see the dark wrought-iron tracery that filled the gap between the columns.

'Paul, the gates. They've been closed!'

They had indeed been closed and moreover fastened with a chain and heavy padlock.

Temple concealed his sense of danger. He did not need to look at Steve to know that she was frightened. The whole series of events made it evident that they had been drawn into some sort of a trap: the silent derelict house, the cries of the

145

bound and gagged Tony Wyman, the fire, the immobilised car and now the locked gates.

'There must be some other way out,' he said, with more assurance than he felt. He went to examine the fence on the left-hand side of the gates. It was of metal mesh and about seven feet high. By comparison with everything else at Breakwater House it was in new condition.

'What's on the other side, Steve?'

'A high wire fence,' she called back a moment later.

'I suppose I could try and climb over—' Temple stood back, measuring the height with his eye.

'No, Paul! Please don't try. Let's walk round and see if there's another way out.'

They were just starting to walk along the inside of the fence towards Seadale when the tops of the trees above them were swept by a pale light. Steve clutched Temple's arm, but he gripped her hand reassuringly.

'It's a car coming. Someone must have seen the fire. We'll wait by the gates.'

The car approached at speed and they could hear the underside of the chassis scraping on the road as it wallowed over the potholes. It drew up at the gates, its headlights shining through the ironwork on to the faces of Temple and Steve. The car doors opened but, dazzled by the glare, Temple could not see who had got out till two men walked forward, their bodies silhouetted but their faces indistinguishable.

'Hello, Temple!' Temple recognised the voice as Mike Langdon's. 'I'm sorry we're late.'

'Why, hello, Langdon,' he said, with surprise.

'George Kelburn's there, too,' Steve murmured. She had recognised George Kelburn by his ample figure, confident walk and the slightly aggressive set of his head. He came forward now into the full light of the headlamps.

'Good evening, Temple. I'm sorry we're late but we had a devil of a job finding this place. Why on earth did you ask us to meet you here?'

'I asked you to meet me here?' Temple repeated in astonishment.

'Yes.'

'When?'

'What do you mean – when?' Kelburn demanded impatiently. 'You sent me a note just as I was finishing dinner.'

Langdon, realising that the lights were dazzling the Temples, had gone back to the car. He switched the headlights off, but left the sidelights burning.

'And the note said . . .?'

'The note asked me to meet you here – tonight.' Kelburn was obviously excessively irritated. 'It said you had some information for me about my wife – although why in heaven's name you should ask me to meet you at a God-forsaken place like this, I can't imagine!'

'Kelburn – I didn't send that note – I didn't ask you to meet me here . . .'

'You didn't? Then who on earth did?'

'Say, wait a minute!' Langdon exclaimed. 'What's going on up the avenue there? Is it a fire, Temple?'

'Yes,' Steve said, 'and Tony Wyman's very badly hurt – he needs a doctor. It's urgent.'

'Tony Wyman! Is he here?' Kelburn's suspicious mind was already jumping to conclusions. 'Is that what you were going to tell me, Temple? That you'd discovered that Tony Wyman and my wife were having . . .'

'I wasn't going to tell you anything!' Temple did not

147

conceal his exasperation. 'I've already told you, I didn't send that note . . .'

'Well, somebody did!'

'Look, Mr Kelburn,' Steve said, a note of urgency in her voice. 'Wyman's very seriously hurt. He needs a doctor!'

Langdon showed more concern for Tony Wyman than Kelburn. 'Where is he, Mrs Temple?'

'He's up near the house. We had to leave him there.'

'I'll drive back into the village,' Langdon said, moving towards the car. 'Will you stay here with Mr and Mrs Temple, sir?'

'Yes, all right! But don't be long, Langdon.'

'And 'phone the Fire Brigade . . .' Temple called after him.

Langdon slammed the car door and started his engine. He had to reverse several times, but finally he straightened the car and drove off towards Seadale.

'Can I join you, Temple, or is this gate locked?'

'It's locked.' Temple pointed to the padlock.

'There must be a way through.' Kelburn was not the kind of man to be stopped by a mere padlock and chain. 'Let's take a look at the fence.'

'We've already looked at the fence,' Temple assured him, staying where he was as Kelburn moved along on the outside of the fence, peering at the ground. He had gone about twenty yards when he straightened up and called back:

'Temple, come over here. It seems to be looser just along here. Maybe if you lifted the wire I could crawl through and join you.'

'Yes, all right,' Temple said resignedly. There was no point in Kelburn trying to get in. It was just that the man could not bear to be frustrated by any obstacle and had to prove that he could overcome it.

He was picking his way towards the spot where Kelburn was waiting impatiently when behind him Steve shouted, 'Paul – wait!'

'What is it, Steve?'

'Look, Paul! Here, where I'm shining the torch . . .'

Temple went back to where she was stooping over a small furry body, its head and one paw trapped in the mesh of the fence.

'A dead squirrel. It's been caught in the wire, by the look of things.'

'Yes, but that wouldn't have killed it! Look at its coat – it's all scorched.'

Temple, his mind racing, cast a glance back towards the power-house in the wood. 'That means that the fence must be electrified! Don't touch that fence, Kelburn!'

'Don't touch it, Mr Kelburn!' Steve echoed. 'It's electrified!'

Kelburn withdrew his hand as swiftly as if he had actually received a shock. 'Phew! That was a damned near thing, Temple. I was just going to lift it up . . .'

'Paul, that's what Wyman meant – he must have known Mr Kelburn was coming here. He told us to warn him.'

'What do you mean, Mrs Temple?' Kelburn, shaken, had come close enough to hear what she said.

'Tony Wyman told us to warn you about the fence,' Steve explained. 'He said: Don't let Kelburn touch it . . .'

'Wyman said that?'

'Yes.'

'But how did Wyman know I was coming here? Did you tell him I was coming, Temple?'

'I've told you.' Temple was really angry now, partly because Kelburn's obstinacy had nearly killed him. 'I *didn't know* you were coming!'

'Yes, of course.' Kelburn was sobered by the anger in Temple's voice. 'I wonder if it was Wyman that sent that note?'

'If he sent the note, then obviously it was a trap to get you here.'

'That's what I mean!'

'Then why did he warn you about the fence?'

'The thing that puzzles me, Temple,' said Sir Graham Forbes, leaning forward and putting his elbows on the desk, 'is why did Tony Wyman go to Breakwater House in the first place? It's obvious he went there to meet someone, but who was it?'

'I can't answer that question, Sir Graham.'

Temple and Raine were sitting in the armchairs facing Sir Graham. It was a little before midday on the following day. The weather had taken a turn for the worse and a squally wind was driving rain against the windows of the Scotland Yard building.

'Could it have been you, Temple?' Raine suggested. He was in a prickly mood, slightly suspicious of Temple's uncanny ability to steal a march on the CID. The Superintendent believed that crimes were solved by methodical and painstaking police methods and he could not help feeling a certain resentment at the way in which Forbes deferred to Paul Temple.

'What do you mean by that, Superintendent?' Temple asked with a frown.

Raine realised he had gone too far. 'Well,' he hedged, 'from what you've told us he seemed to be expecting you to turn up.'

'Yes, I agree that he wasn't in the least surprised to see me. But that doesn't necessarily mean that he went to the house to meet me.'

'I'm not sure,' Raine persisted. 'Perhaps Kelburn wasn't the only person who received a note with your name on it.'

Forbes was watching the exchange between the two men, aware of the tension that had built up between them.

'That's certainly a point, Raine,' he interposed tactfully. 'Did you see the note, Temple?'

'Yes. It was signed with my name, but it wasn't my signature. In fact, it could have been written by either Kelburn or Langdon, just to explain their presence at the house. Incidentally, what was the latest report on Wyman?'

'Not very healthy, I'm afraid,' Raine said. 'Apparently he had a heart condition, even before—'

'Not very surprising,' Forbes commented, 'when you consider he's had two attempts on his life in less than a week. Come in!'

The last words were directed at the door, which opened to admit a young, fresh-faced man of about thirty-five. He had a trim, fit figure and a carefully clipped beard.

'May I come in, Sir Graham?'

'Come along in, Burton.' Forbes rose from his chair. 'Good of you to come up. Temple, this is Detective-Inspector Burton, Brighton CID.'

'Good morning, Inspector.' Temple too had stood up. He offered Burton his hand.

'Mr Temple.' Burton's hand-clasp was strong and his expression was deferential. 'I'm very pleased to meet you, sir.'

He and Raine exchanged a brief nod of greeting. The Superintendent had not risen from his chair. He said: 'Any news of Fiona Scott?'

'No trace of her, Superintendent. She left her digs after getting Mr Temple's 'phone call last night. We're still making enquiries.'

Temple felt Raine's eyes on him and knew that he was being blamed for the disappearance of this important informant.

Burton handed Forbes the envelope he was carrying. 'However, I thought this might interest you, sir.'

'What is it?'

'It's a report on the fingerprints we found at Breakwater House. One set has been identified as belonging to a man called Harris. Midge Harris. You remember Midge Harris, Superintendent? He was picked up.'

'Midge Harris?' Forbes had not opened the envelope. 'Surely he's in prison—'

'That's right, sir. We pulled him in about three weeks ago. He was mixed up in the Regent Street smash-and-grab.'

'The loot's still missing, isn't it?'

'That's right, Inspector,' Forbes confirmed. 'Silver plate and jewellery, about a million pounds' worth.'

'But I remember Midge Harris,' Temple said. 'Short, red-haired little chap. He was one of the small fry in the Safe Deposit affair. You say he was picked up about three weeks ago, Superintendent?'

Forbes answered the question. 'It was while you were in America, Temple. We have him sewn up this time. He was identified by four witnesses, including the jeweller.'

Temple stared thoughtfully out of the window for a moment. 'Obviously he must have been in Breakwater House some time ago. Sir Graham, do you think I could have a word with him?'

'You're wasting your time, Mr Temple,' Raine said at once. 'Midge won't talk, even if he knows anything. I had six hours with him the day he was arrested and he was as tight as a clam.'

'All the same, I'd like—'

Temple was interrupted by the shrilling of the telephone on the desk. With a look of apology Forbes went to pick it up. He spoke briefly, then held out the receiver to Burton. 'It's for you. Sergeant Wetherall.'

Burton took the 'phone. 'Hello, Sergeant.' He listened for a few seconds, nodding several times. 'When did it happen? . . . I see . . . Well, you know what to do. The usual drill . . . I'll see you this evening.'

As he replaced the receiver his face did not change.

'Bad news, I'm afraid, Sir Graham. Tony Wyman died this morning without regaining consciousness.'

At about the same time as Temple was hearing about Tony Wyman's death Steve was hanging up some dresses in the wardrobe of her husband's dressing-room. Charlie had gone out to do some shopping, so when she heard the doorbell ring she went to answer it herself.

'Why, Laura!'

'Hello, Steve. May I come in?'

Laura Kelburn was wearing a Burberry raincoat which was still gleaming wet after the recent shower. She'd put a headscarf over her hair.

'Yes, of course.' Recovering from her surprise, Steve held the door back. 'Do come in. Would you like to take your raincoat off?'

Laura was grateful for the warm welcome. She took her Burberry off and watched Steve put it on a hanger.

'I happened to be passing, and I thought perhaps I . . .' She stopped and then appeared to change her mind. 'No, that's not true. Steve, I want a word with your husband. I realise he probably hates being interrupted at work but . . .'

'I'm sorry, but he's out, Laura. He's at Scotland Yard.'

'Oh. What time will he be back, do you know?'

'No, I'm afraid I don't. It may not be until this evening. But come into the sitting-room.'

Laura was still nervous as she preceded Steve into the room. 'You – you've been away, haven't you?'

'Yes, we went down to Brighton for a few days.'

'Yes, I know. I telephoned. I – I left a message.'

'We got the message, Laura – the same day. There was really nothing to worry about.'

'Oh. Oh, good.' Laura's anxious expression relaxed a little. At Steve's invitation she sat down. It was evident that there was something she wanted to talk about.

'I gather there's some trouble between you and your husband?' Steve prompted helpfully.

'That's putting it mildly.' Laura laughed uneasily. 'Things have been impossible just lately – quite impossible. He's so jealous, it just isn't true! Darling, may I have a cigarette?'

'Yes, of course. There's some on the table beside you. Help yourself.'

Laura took a cigarette from the silver box and lit it with the lighter standing beside it.

'He's always imagining I'm having an affair with some younger man,' she said from behind a cloud of smoke.

Steve gazed back at her frankly. 'Do you have affairs with younger men, Laura?'

'Now, don't be idiotic! What do you take me for? George gives me everything I want. Why should I stick my neck out like that?'

'Well, we did see you in a sports Alfa Romeo with Larry Cross one evening.'

'Larry Cross?' Laura repeated the name as if it was totally unknown to her.

154

'Dr Benkaray's secretary. Paul and I saw you a couple of nights ago. The two of you were in a red Alfa . . .'

'A red . . .?' Laura puckered up her brow and made a great effort to remember. 'Yes, of course! I remember now! Oh, so his name's Cross, is it? I didn't know. I knew he was the doctor's secretary, of course, otherwise I wouldn't have accepted a lift from him.'

'He was just giving you a lift?'

'That's right.' Laura was in her stride and more confident now. 'I'd been to the cinema in Curzon Street and couldn't get a taxi. Suddenly he popped up and offered me a lift. I was delighted.'

'But you didn't know who he was?' said Steve, still sceptical.

'I've told you, I knew he was the doctor's secretary but I didn't know his name.'

'How did you know he was Dr Benkaray's secretary, then?'

'Because I've been to see the doctor myself. This man – Larry Cross, did you say his name was? – makes the appointments.'

'Why did you go and see Dr Benkaray, Laura?'

'I say, what is this – an inquisition?' Laura laughed again, making a joke of it. 'If you must know, I was nervy – on edge – couldn't sleep. It's really not surprising after all I've been through just lately.'

'Did you know that Julia consulted Dr Benkaray?'

'Yes.' Laura suddenly became serious. Her face sagged as she abandoned the attempt at levity. 'And that's how I came to go there myself. Julia raved about her.'

'What was she treating Julia for, do you know?'

'Yes, I know, but I swore I wouldn't . . .' Having taken no more than half a dozen puffs she stubbed the cigarette out in an ashtray. 'Well, I suppose now that Julia's dead there's no reason why you shouldn't know. Julia was taking heroin. Dr Benkaray was trying to cure her of the habit.'

'I see. Laura, tell me, is it just since Julia died that things have become difficult between you and your husband?'

'They've come to the surface more, if that's what you mean. Things have been particularly difficult, I suppose, since Mike Langdon arrived. I sometimes wonder if he puts ideas into George's head.'

'Why should he do that?'

'Well, he's seen me at The Hide and Seek once or twice, talking to Tony Wyman. By the way, I read about Tony this morning. Is he badly hurt?'

'Yes, I'm afraid he is.'

'Was he conscious when you found him?' Laura asked, so obviously curious that Steve suspected that the purpose of her visit was to find out what Tony Wyman had said to them.

'He was unconscious most of the time,' she said, which was perfectly true. 'Is that what you wanted to see Paul about – Tony Wyman?'

'No, no, it was something quite different. I've already told you most of it.'

'Then why not tell me the rest?'

'It's just this, Steve. I happened to overhear a conversation between my husband and Mike Langdon. Mike was telling George that your husband was the best man to get the evidence – against me – for the divorce.'

Steve laughed. 'But Paul doesn't go in for that sort of thing, you must know that!'

'George has a way of persuading people.'

'Don't worry, Laura. It would take more than money to persuade my husband to do something he doesn't want to do!'

*

156

In his work as an author and consultant on crime, Paul Temple had regular contacts with a number of crime reporters on the big newspapers. One of these was Ken Sinclair of the *Evening World*. Temple had advised him about many of the cases he had been following up and made available his encyclopaedic knowledge of the world of crime. In return, Ken had frequently kept him informed of the day-to-day gossip and inside information which are the lifeblood of a crime reporter.

He 'phoned Ken at his home – he was never at the paper till the afternoon – and made an appointment to meet him in a Fleet Street pub for a bar lunch.

Ken was at the Crown and Anchor before he was, his tall, thin frame bent over the bar as he stared thoughtfully into half a pint of beer. He was oblivious to the babble of conversation in the crowded saloon. With his long hair and aesthete's features he looked more like a university don than a reporter and his unconventional, casual dress reinforced that impression.

He greeted Temple warmly, ordered him a Scotch and soda, enquired briefly about his trip to the United States and then got down to business. 'Well – what's it all about? What can I do for you?'

'Ken, while I was in America there was a smash-and-grab in Regent Street. The police arrested a man called Midge Harris.'

'That's right.'

'Give me the low-down. What exactly happened?'

'Well, whoever did the job got away with a considerable amount of jewellery. Midge was in on it – there's no doubt about that, he was identified – but Midge was just one of the boys. He certainly wasn't the brains behind the set-up. You know Midge Harris, he's as clever as paint, but he's smalltime.'

'Who do you think was behind it?'

Ken slid his glass along the counter to make way for a customer who was pushing in to have four tankards refilled with bitter.

'Why, this character they call The Fence. I don't think there's any doubt he was behind the operation. Let's face it, he's behind most of the crime these days. You see, the whole point is – the boys know that the moment they've pulled a job the stuff will be taken off their hands and they'll be paid good money for it.'

'But there's nothing new about this, Ken – there have always been fences.'

'Yes, but not one like this, this chap's really got things organised. He operates on an international scale – will handle anything. But why are you interested in Midge Harris and The Fence? I thought you were investigating the Kelburn murder.'

'I am.'

'You think there's a connection?' Ken's interest was aroused.

'There could be.' Temple knew Ken would understand his reticence, knowing that as soon as the story broke he would be the first to hear. 'Ken, tell me about Midge Harris. What's he been doing during the past two or three years?'

'He had a job with a transport firm for a time, but it was only a cover for his more nefarious activities, I'm sure of that. He's been living with a girl called Sally Jackson. Strange girl – she used to be an art student, then she started a ladies' hairdressers in Camden Town.'

'How long have they been together?'

'About three or four years. I don't quite know what she saw in Midge. She was a very much better class of person than he was . . . Listen, I think we'd better order some food before this pack of wolves cleans the place out.'

*

Temple had visited prisons many times before and they never failed to depress him. It was not just the chilling sensation of being trapped when the heavy doors closed behind you, nor that distinctive aroma, part scent, part stink, that was compounded of human bodies, disinfectant and soap. What really got him down was the sense of waste, all these human beings lost to society, many of them with exceptional gifts. No wonder the warder who showed him up to the Governor's office, a kindly man to judge by his face, wore a permanently sad expression.

Raine was there already and could not refrain from glancing at the clock on the wall. It was ten minutes after five, the time of his appointment. No one else was in the room, which had the crisp, efficient air of a military commander's headquarters. Temple was not surprised to see a photograph on the wall of some regiment receiving colours from the Queen. Incongruously, a vase of fresh spring flowers stood on the Governor's desk.

'I'm sorry I'm late, Superintendent, but I've had rather a busy day.'

'That's all right.' Raine was off-hand. 'I've spoken to the Governor – they're fetching Harris now.'

'Good. Incidentally, I went to see a girl named Sally Jackson this morning.'

'Midge's girlfriend?' Raine said, unimpressed.

'Oh, so you know?'

'Yes.' Raine spoke with a degree of self-satisfaction. 'She wasn't at home, of course.'

'No, she was in the South of France, from what I was able to gather.'

Temple's expedition out to Camden Town had taken a long time and been unrewarding. He had walked miles tracking down the address Ken Sinclair had given him and when he found the ladies' hairdressing salon it was closed and the blinds drawn. He tried the knocker of the front door beside it and after his second, more imperative knock it was opened by a slatternly woman. Sally Jackson, the woman told him, had left for Nice a fortnight ago, and had asked her to look after the place. Sally had left no forwarding address nor had she given any indication of when she might return.

'The South of France?' Raine chuckled. 'That's near enough. Soon after we picked up Midge, Sally suddenly came into money and decided to travel.'

'Where did she get the money from, do you know?'

'Well, our bet is someone took care of her in order to stop Midge talking . . .'

Behind Raine the door had opened and a small man with a very erect carriage and a well-trimmed moustache had come in. Despite his size, he had a commanding presence and an easy, confident manner.

'Governor, may I introduce Mr Paul Temple?'

'How do you do, sir,' said Temple.

'How do you do, Mr Temple.' The Governor gave Temple a quick assessing scrutiny and apparently liked what he saw. 'Delighted to meet you. Well, everything's ready, Superintendent. He's in the Chaplain's room.'

'How does he seem?'

'Oh – surly,' the Governor said with resignation. 'I doubt whether he'll be very co-operative.'

'No,' Raine agreed. 'Well – he's all yours, Temple. I wish you luck.'

The Governor opened the door again. 'This way, Mr Temple.'

Midge Harris was waiting uneasily in the Chaplain's room, which had the impersonal air of a place that has several different users, none of whom wants to make it too expressive of his own personality or creed. Midge's spare frame was too small to fill the prison uniform. His red hair, cropped short, gave him an aggressive look and his small eyes were suspicious.

Temple pulled the chair out from behind the table so that he would be on the same side of it as Midge.

'Sit down, Midge. Make yourself comfortable.'

'There ain't no comfort in this place,' Midge said.

'Well, have a cigarette.'

'What's the big idea coming here, Mr Temple? What's the game?'

'No game at all. I played straight enough with you last time, didn't I?'

'Well—' Midge shrugged grudgingly and consented to sit down.

'Light your cigarette and relax. Here—' Temple handed him the packet he had bought for this purpose in Camden Town and struck a match. Midge selected a cigarette and leant forward over the flame.

'First I've had since they shoved me in this stinkin' hole.'

'Yes, it was bad luck being picked up like that. I suppose you did do the job?'

'Is that what you've come to find out? The Beak said I done it.'

'Well, if the Beak said you done it – you done it.' Midge acknowledged the leg-pull with a wry jerk of his head, but he did not smile. 'No, it's nothing to do with that, Midge. I want your help over something else.'

'Oh, yes?'

'Someone tried to murder me the other night.'

'Murder you?' Midge stared at Temple incredulously.

'Yes.'

'Go on – you're kiddin' . . .'

'No, I'm not kidding. It happened near Brighton at a place called Breakwater House. Have you ever been to Breakwater House, Midge?'

At the mention of Breakwater House, Midge's eyes narrowed. He drew hard on his cigarette and blew out a smokescreen. 'No, I 'aven't.'

'Now that surprises me, because they found your finger-prints there, in one of the rooms.'

'Who told you that?'

'Superintendent Raine.'

'He's up the creek!' Midge expostulated. 'How could my prints be at Breakwater House? I been stuck in this stinking place for three weeks.'

'I'm not suggesting that you were there recently, Midge, or that you had anything to do with the attempt on my life.'

'Then what are you suggesting?'

Temple crossed his legs and leant an elbow on the back of his chair. 'That you went to Breakwater House some little time ago and that the person who invited you there was the person who tried to murder me.'

'I don't know what you're talking about.'

'I'm talking about Margo – alias The Fence.'

'I've never 'eard of anyone called Margo.' Midge had tensed up, he kept his eyes on the tip of his cigarette, avoiding Temple's. 'I 'aven't been to Brighton for years.'

'Then how do you account for the fingerprints?'

'I don't know.' Midge ran a hand over the back of his head, rattled by the friendly but insistent questons. 'I can't account for 'em. I expect it's a frame-up – it usually is a bloody frame-up.'

'Midge, I don't want to scare you, but you're mixed up with a pretty ruthless crowd. Now, if I were you . . .'

'Well, you're not me, Mr Temple,' Midge burst out with sudden violence. 'So keep the effing advice to yourself!'

'All right, Midge, if you won't talk I'll have to have another word with your girlfriend, Sally Jackson.'

Temple had stood up. Midge, who seemed even smaller hunched on the chair, blinked up at him.

'What d'yer mean – another word?'

'I saw her this afternoon in that hairdressing salon of hers, but she was working like a slave and she could hardly spare the time to talk to me.'

'You saw her this afternoon? I don't believe you.'

'All right. You don't have to believe me, Midge.'

Midge jumped excitedly to his feet. 'You made a mistake – that wasn't Sal. She's got pots of money now; she's gone abroad somewhere.'

'That's what you think!' Temple contemplated the agitated little crook with an expression of pity. 'When she discovered I was a friend of yours she wanted to borrow fifty quid off me. That doesn't sound as if she's got pots of money, does it?'

When Temple returned to the Governor's office he found the two men engaged in a discussion of the merits of the 'short, sharp, shock' method of dealing with young offenders. They broke off as he came in.

'Well, Temple, any luck?'

'Not much, I'm afraid, Governor. He's a surly little devil, isn't he?'

'Yes,' Raine agreed, 'and I wouldn't trust him as far as I could throw the – the little—'

Temple laughed. 'You mean you wouldn't trust him.'

The Governor stood up, his eyes straying to the pile of correspondence on his desk. 'Well, is there anything else we can do for you, Superintendent?'

'No, thank you, sir. You've been extremely helpful and we're very grateful to you for—'

'Yes, there is one small thing, Governor,' Temple cut in on Raine's effusive thanks, 'if you'd be kind enough.'

'Anything to help, Mr Temple.'

'During the next twenty-four hours a postcard will arrive for Harris – it'll have a little drawing in the right-hand corner. I want you to make sure he gets it, the moment it arrives.'

'Yes, of course, but how do you know—' The Governor stopped as he saw Temple smile. He nodded sagely. 'I think I understand. I won't ask who's going to send it.'

'Sorry, Charlie, I left my key in the study.'

'That's all right, Mr Temple.'

'Mrs Temple in the drawing-room?'

It was after seven and Temple was looking forward to a sherry before dinner.

'No, she's gone out, sir. She went out about half an hour ago.'

'Oh? Where has she gone, do you know?'

'No, she didn't say, but she seemed in quite a flap with . . . quite excited, Mr Temple.'

Charlie helped Temple off with his raincoat and hung it up.

'What do you mean, quite excited?'

'Well, it was just after Mrs Temple made the 'phone call. She came into the kitchen and . . .'

'What 'phone call? Who did Mrs Temple ring up?'

'I don't know, sir.' Charlie was alarmed by the abrupt urgency in Temple's voice. 'I don't know who it was, but about two minutes later Mrs Temple popped into the kitchen and said she was going out.'

'But she didn't say anything else?'

'Oh, yes, sir. She said, "I'm going out, Charlie, but if Mr Temple gets home before I get back just say . . ." Then she said a very funny thing.'

Temple tried to control his impatience. Charlie had this maddening tendency to spill his information into penny packets.

'Well – what did she say?'

'She said just two words, Mr Temple.'

'*What* two words, Charlie?'

Charlie reflected as if he was not sure now if he had remembered right. Then he suggested tentatively:

'Edgar Northampton?'

CHAPTER VII

A Time To Worry

Steve had been in the study writing out some cheques when she'd heard the doorbell ring. It was a time of day when Charlie usually retired to his room – he was a compulsive listener to *Woman's Hour* – and with his radio turned up he was deaf to all other sounds. When, after a long pause, the bell rang again, she went to answer it herself, half expecting to find Laura Kelburn on the doorstep again. But this visitor was a good deal less poised and confident. Mrs Fletcher was wearing a new red Marks and Spencer's overcoat and a hat more suitable for a woman twenty years younger. She was very diffident and nervous.

'Mrs Temple?'

'Yes.'

'I'd like a word with your husband, Mrs Temple. Do you think I could possibly . . . Oh, I beg your pardon – I don't think we've met. My name is Fletcher, I met your husband down at Westerton.'

'I'm very sorry, but my husband isn't in just at the moment. I'm expecting him back, though, if you'd care to wait.'

'Oh, dear! I thought this might happen. I should have 'phoned of course, and made an appointment.'

'You can leave a message, Mrs Fletcher.'

'Well, I – I wanted to see your husband personally.' Mrs Fletcher's manner changed, she became almost accusing.

'You see, Mrs Temple, your husband called at the garage – he questioned my son, Bill.'

'Yes, I know. Look, hadn't you better come in? I'm expecting my husband back at any moment.'

Mrs Fletcher declined to remove hat or coat, and she insisted on Steve preceding her into the sitting-room.

'Bill's a good boy, he's as straight as a die. He has nothing to do with this business – nothing at all.'

'Which business are you referring to?'

'I'm talking about the murder – about Julia Kelburn.' Quite happy to repeat herself, she insisted: 'Bill doesn't know anything about it – nothing at all.'

'Do you know anything about it, Mrs Fletcher?'

'That's not the point,' Mrs Fletcher said belligerently. 'It's my boy I'm concerned with – he's the one I'm worried about at the moment. Now, you tell Mr Temple to leave him alone! There's no reason for your husband, or anyone else, to question Bill.'

'My husband has to question quite a lot of people who are not directly involved,' Steve said reasonably. 'He always works that way. That helps him to decide which people are really implicated.'

'Yes, well, you tell him to leave Bill alone.'

'All right, Mrs Fletcher, I'll do that. But I think you're making a great mistake. My husband likes your son – he's already told me so.'

'Then why did he question him like that?'

'He wanted to know what Bill knew about Dr Benkaray and your relationship with the doctor.'

'That's no concern of your husband's!'

'I think it is. Look, Mrs Fletcher, I don't know why you should feel particularly unfriendly towards my husband, wasn't it you who warned us about the parcel from the dress shop?'

'Yes, it was,' Mrs Fletcher admitted. Steve guessed that she would find it difficult to tell a lie. But the reminder of that telephone call unsettled her. 'Look, Mrs Temple, I must go now. I'm sorry if I've been rude.'

'That's all right.'

'I'm flying to Australia in two or three days' time.' Mrs Fletcher was moving towards the door. 'So I don't expect I shall see—'

'Australia? Is your son going with you?'

'No, I'm leaving him behind. I think he'll stand a better chance on his own. The garage business is all in order and I've made it over to him.'

'I see.'

Mrs Fletcher turned and came back a few paces. She wagged a finger warningly at Steve.

'But in case Dr Benkaray and her crowd ever try to drag my son into anything, I wanted Mr Temple to know that Bill isn't that sort. He's straight as an arrow is Bill.'

'What exactly are you suggesting they might drag him into, Mrs Fletcher? It would be as well for my husband to know, if you want him to keep a friendly eye on your son.'

'They're mixed up in all sorts of things, Mrs Temple,' said Mrs Fletcher, with another abrupt change of mood. 'Stolen property, drugs . . . All I ever did was to pass on messages or deliver packages that looked innocent enough. But I was a fool – I ought to have realised that they couldn't have paid that sort of money simply for running errands. I should have packed it in months ago.'

'Have you ever met the person behind all this – the person they call Margo?'

'Margo? The person who controls the outfit is The Fence, Mrs Temple. The name Margo is just for identification purposes.'

'What do you mean?'

'I'm sorry, but I can't give you any more information.'

'No, wait a moment!' Steve had stayed where she was, in the middle of the room. It was difficult to leave when your hostess stands her ground and Mrs Fletcher paused on the threshold. 'Tell me one thing, Mrs Fletcher, before you go. Do these people – the people you've been working for – know that you're going away?'

'No, I don't think so.'

'Well, supposing they find out and bring pressure to bear on your son?'

'They won't do that, Mrs Temple. You see, if they try to get Bill involved I should go straight to the police. I've told them that.'

'Yes, but they could – well—'

'I've warned them not to try anything with me, either. I've got certain documents and tape recordings in a very safe place. If anything should happen to me they'll pass into the right hands. Bill will see to that all right.'

When she had closed the door on Mrs Fletcher, who had barely been in the house five minutes, Steve stood in the hall, thinking. She was trying to remember exactly what Bill Fletcher had told Paul. She repeated the phrase aloud to see if it sounded right. 'If Dr Benkaray gets difficult, just say two words to her: "Edgar Northampton".'

She snapped her fingers, determined to find out if her hunch was correct. Her watch told her that it was only three o'clock so the banks were still open. Her 'phone call to the bank where she and Temple had their accounts was answered by a clerk. No, he said, the manager was not available, he was with a customer.

'Tell him Mrs Temple will be coming in at – in half an hour,' Steve said firmly. 'It's vitally important that I see him! It's a matter of life and death!'

When Steve let herself into the flat about three hours later she was astonished to see Charlie and Temple rush out of the kitchen and drawing-room respectively. You'd have thought from their expressions that she'd just made a successful parachute landing after a ten-thousand-foot free-fall.

'Steve! Where on earth have you been?'

'Hello, Paul!' Steve greeted her husband casually. 'Take my coat, Charlie, will you?'

'Certainly, Mrs Temple,' said Charlie, darting forward.

'Steve, what the devil did you mean by—'

'You look worried, Paul. Is anything the matter?'

'Of course I'm worried! Leaving mysterious messages and disappearing like that—'

'Come into the drawing-room, darling, and I'll tell you all about it. But first will you mix me a dry martini? I've had quite a day.'

'You've had—' Temple began, then thought better of it. He mixed Steve's drink and freshened up his own Scotch and soda. 'Now, Steve, what's all this about? Where have you been?'

Steve sat down, crossed her legs and sipped her drink gratefully. 'You remember what Mrs Fletcher said to Mike

Langdon: "If Dr Benkaray gets difficult just say two words to her – Edgar Northampton". . .'

'Yes.'

'Well, I've discovered what she meant.'

'What did she mean?'

'Shall I start at the beginning?'

'I don't care where you start – providing you tell me what this is all about!'

Temple listened carefully while she told him about Mrs Fletcher's visit.

'After she left I remembered what you'd told me about Edgar Northampton, and it suddenly dawned on me that the documents she'd referred to were probably in a deed box at his bank. So I telephoned Reggie Whiteside . . .'

'At the bank?'

'Yes. I asked if he could see me. He was in a meeting, but I said it was a matter of life and death, so—'

'By Timothy, you really are the limit, Steve!' There was more admiration than rebuke in Temple's comment.

'Anyway, I saw Reggie and I asked him if he could find out whether a Mrs Fletcher had deposited a deed box at the bank in Tenterhurst.'

Temple shook his head in amazement.

'He telephoned Northampton and said an enquiry had come through about the garage in Westerton, and he wondered if the bank held the deeds. Northampton said they didn't but that Mrs Fletcher had certainly deposited a deed box with them some little time ago.'

'I see.' Temple contemplated his wife thoughtfully. The anger which had been caused by his anxiety for her safety had evaporated. 'But the banks close at half past three. What kept you so long?'

'It was nearly half past four when I left Reggie. Then I went round by Curzon Street to check up on something Laura Kelburn told me.'

'Laura? Has she been here, too?'

Steve filled Temple in on Laura's visit. 'My impression was,' she finished, 'that it was an excuse to find out if Tony Wyman had told us anything. Is there any news on him, by the way?'

'Yes. He died this morning without regaining consciousness.'

'Oh, no!' Steve was genuinely sad. 'Poor Tony. He had such talent and I can't understand how he got mixed up in all this.'

'Drugs, almost certainly. But, to go back to Edgar Northampton, it's your deduction that the deed box contains a great deal more than just the deeds of the garage?'

'Well, what do you think?'

'I think you're right, Steve.' Temple slapped his knees and stood up. 'I think you're a hundred per cent right – but in future, young woman, please let me do the investigating around here!'

Steve laughed. 'All right, but thank you for the word "young", anyway.'

'I want you to do something for me, Steve.' Paul had gone to the writing bureau in the window embrasure and was rummaging about in it. 'Where are the postcards, darling?'

'On the left of the writing paper.'

'Ah, yes. Here we are. Steve, you were always pretty good at drawing. I want you to sketch a girl's head on the back of this postcard. Here you are, dear, use my pen.'

Steve took the postcard, at a loss to understand what on earth he had in his mind. 'A girl's head?'

'Yes, just a rough drawing, Steve, showing a girl's head under a dryer at the hairdresser's.'

'You don't want much!'

'It doesn't matter how rough it is,' Paul told her encouragingly. Temple knew that she would do a better drawing if he was not looking over her shoulder. He went out to the 'cellar' he kept in a cupboard near the kitchen, selected a bottle of good claret and drew the cork. During the half hour he had been waiting for Steve to come back he'd had time to think what life would be like without her. Even though she had been in no real danger her safe return was surely a matter for celebration. When he went back into the sitting-room Steve had finished her sketch. She held it up for him to inspect.

'Will that do?'

'Oh, that's very good, Steve.' He gave a shout for Charlie, then leant over Steve's chair. 'Now write underneath: "So much for your friends. Still sweating my guts out. Sal."'

'That's a bit crude, isn't it?'

'Midge isn't exactly the sophisticated type,' Paul murmured.

'Who?'

'Never mind. Just write what I told you.'

Before she had finished writing the message, Charlie had appeared in answer to Temple's summons.

'Hang on a minute, Charlie, I want you to post something for me. It's all right, Steve, I'll print the address.'

As he took the postcard over to the writing bureau the telephone started to ring.

'I'll take it, Paul,' Steve said.

He nodded, concentrating on printing the address in crude capitals, not listening to Steve's end of the conversation. When it was finished to his satisfaction he handed it to the patiently waiting Charlie.

'Right, Charlie. Now, go down to Camden Town—'

'Camden Town?' Charlie repeated, unable to believe his ears.

'Yes. Camden Town. And post this in the first letter box you see.'

'What about your dinner, Mr Temple?'

'Put it in the hostess trolley and we'll help ourselves.'

'Okay, Mr Temple.'

Not at all happy with the assignment, Charlie glanced at Steve, but she was holding the telephone away from her ear, a hand over the mouthpiece. Charlie turned and slowly went out.

'It's George Kelburn, Paul. He wants us to go over and have a drink this evening. He's very affable and friendly all of a sudden. What shall I say?'

'Kelburn?'

'Yes. He says he's particularly anxious to have a chat with you.'

'Tell him we'd be delighted,' Temple said, making up his mind. 'We'll be there at –' He glanced at his watch. 'About nine.'

When Steve had relayed the message and replaced the receiver she looked up to see her husband staring into his empty glass as if he was wondering where the whisky had disappeared to.

'What is it, Paul? Is anything wrong?'

'I wonder why Kelburn wants to see us?'

It was Mike Langdon who opened the door of the house, and he was evidently in high spirits.

'Nice to see you, Temple. Glad you could both make it.'

'I thought you'd be on your way back to New York by now.'

'No, no, not yet.' Langdon was helping Steve off with her coat. 'I'm keeping my fingers crossed. Any moment now, with a bit of luck.'

'There's been a change in the situation?' Temple guessed.

'There certainly has!' said Langdon, grinning. 'Kelburn's had a change of heart. He's decided he's still very much in love with his wife and he's made it up with her.'

'When did this happen?'

'Within the last twenty-four hours. Don't ask me to explain it, it's a mystery to me. Right now you wouldn't think they'd ever seriously considered leaving each other for a weekend, let alone parting for good. Still, I'm all for it! It's a wonderful idea – especially if it gets me back to New York!'

Laura had appeared through a door on the ground floor. She had changed for dinner and was wearing a black dress with a string of pearls encircling her throat. Like Langdon she was full of the joys of spring.

'Hello, Steve! How lovely to see you, my dear!' Impulsively she went to Steve and gave her a kiss on the cheek.

'Good evening, Laura,' Steve murmured, surprised at the change in her manner.

'Hello, Mr Temple. How sweet of you to come!' She turned to Langdon. 'Is George in the drawing-room?'

'I think so, Laura.'

'Come along, then. Let's go in.' Leading the way she opened the drawing-room door, calling out: 'George, our guests have arrived.'

George Kelburn was putting down the evening paper and getting up from his chair as Steve came in. He was wearing a velvet smoking-jacket and a black bow tie. His manner, like Laura's, was festive and genial.

'Ah, good evening, Mrs Temple! How very nice to see you! Temple, my dear fellow, how are you?' To reinforce his welcome Kelburn shook hands warmly with both of them. 'So glad you could make it at such short notice. Mike, will you see to the drinks?'

While the obedient Langdon was ascertaining what the visitors would like to drink, Kelburn assigned them to the chairs where he wanted them to sit. Even in his own drawing-room he needed to feel that he was totally in control of the situation. Laura herself was directed to the chair beside Temple with a commanding little wave of the hand. But he himself remained standing.

'Temple, I owe you an apology,' he announced with a smile.

'An apology?'

'Yes. I'm afraid I've wasted a lot of your valuable time – getting you involved in family affairs which don't concern you. Naturally, I shall see that you're not the loser financially, but that's not the point.'

'What is the point, Kelburn?' Temple responded with equal affability.

Beaming at his wife, Kelburn said: 'Laura and I have decided to forget the past and make a fresh start.'

'I'm delighted to hear it.' Temple tried to show pleasurable surprise even though Langdon had already announced the good tidings.

'I ought never to have doubted her in the first place, I know, but . . .' Kelburn was still gazing at Laura as if he had just discovered her.

'Things haven't been too easy for me just lately.' Kelburn squared his shoulders bravely. 'What with Julia and . . .'

'Darling, we understand,' Laura said.

'Yes, I know you do, my dear – but I wanted Mr and Mrs Temple to realise that I – well – that I'm sorry I ever doubted you, Laura.'

Having made his public declaration, Kelburn went over to his wife, bent down and kissed her on the forehead.

'That's very sweet of you, darling. Now you've said your little piece we'll all drink to it.'

During this idyllic scene Langdon had been pouring out a Scotch and soda for Temple and Kelburn, a Grand Marnier for Steve and a brandy and ginger ale for Laura. He himself was having a Scotch on the rocks. There was a short pause while he handed the tray round. Both Temple and Steve were slightly embarrassed by the couple's demonstrative declaration of affection.

It was Langdon who broke the awkward silence. 'Well, Laura – George – here's to both of you. I can't tell you how glad I am that everything's straightened out.'

'You're just a line-shooter, Mike,' Laura laughed. 'You just want to get back to little old New York, that's all you want!'

'Whatever gave you that idea?' Langdon asked, with mock surprise.

'Why don't you come along with us, Mike?' Kelburn suggested, with a straight face.

'I thought you said this was going to be a second honeymoon, darling.'

Kelburn laughed at Laura's protest. 'I'm only joking, Laura.'

Temple tasted his whisky, and asked casually: 'Are you going away, Mr Kelburn?'

'Yes, we're going on a cruise.' Kelburn at last sat down. He had reserved for himself the big armchair on whose arm the paper lay folded. 'We fixed it up last night, didn't we, Laura? We sail from Southampton at the end of the month.'

'What's the ship?' Temple asked, polite rather than curious.

Kelburn raised his glass in a silent toast to Laura. 'It's an American ship, the *Wisconsin*. It goes to Jamaica and the Caribbean. We'll be away about six months.'

'How wonderful!' Steve gave Temple a meaningful glance. 'I've always wanted to go to Jamaica.'

'Does Sir Graham know about this trip?' Temple enquired.

'No, I haven't told him. We only knew ourselves last night.'

'I think I'd have a word with him, Kelburn. The file on your daughter's case is by no means closed. They may want to get in touch with you.'

'But that's the whole point of taking this cruise!' Laura chided Temple. 'George wants to forget about the whole thing, he wants to get away from Sir Graham Forbes and Superintendent Raine and people like that.'

Having made his point Temple did not labour the matter. The conversation drifted away to foreign travel, Temple's recent tour of the United States and Laura's preference for ocean cruises rather than air travel. At about ten thirty Temple caught Steve's eye and she seized the next gap in the conversation to gather her handbag and stand up.

On the drive home Temple was so silent that Steve asked: 'Is anything wrong, darling?'

'No. I was just thinking, that's all.'

'So was I. Have you ever seen such a change in people? Even Mike Langdon was good fun. And Laura – well, she was positively human, for once. I expect it's the thought of going to Jamaica. Paul, do you think we might—'

'Maybe you're right,' said Temple, in no mood to discuss Steve's holiday plans. 'You know, I find this sudden departure of everybody a little worrying, Steve. The Kelburns going to Jamaica, Langdon returning to New York, Mrs Fletcher off to Australia. I wonder if Dr Benkaray has any plans for going abroad?'

'Good morning. Dr Benkaray's surgery. Can I help you?'

'Is that her – secretary?'

'Yes.'

'Mr Cross?'

'Who's that speaking?'

179

'This is Paul Temple. I'd like a word with Dr Benkaray.'

'I'm sorry, but Dr Benkaray's got several appointments this morning and can't be disturbed.'

'I see. Well, do you think I could speak to her later today – possibly this evening?'

'Yes, I should imagine so. You could ring about half past seven.'

'Thank you. Tell Dr Benkaray we now know who murdered Julia Kelburn, but there's just one small point I'd like to check with the doctor. It won't take a minute. Good—'

'No, hold on! . . . Are you still there, Mr Temple? I'll see if the doctor can spare you a minute.'

'Thank you very much, that's very kind of you.'

Temple held the receiver tight against his right ear and stopped the left one with a finger. He could hear a muttered conversation going on at the Wimpole Street end, but was unable to make out the words. It was a full minute before Dr Benkaray came on the line.

'Good morning, Mr Temple. I understand you wish to speak to me?'

'Oh, good morning, Dr Benkaray. How very kind of you. Yes, I wanted to have a word with you, Doctor, before you left, and just check up on—'

'Before I left?'

'Yes. You are going away, aren't you, Doctor?'

'Yes, as a matter of fact, I am – but how did you know?'

'Oh, I thought it was common knowledge. My wife overheard someone say something about it at a party – one of your patients, I imagine.'

'I see.'

'Where are you going to, Doctor?'

'I'm going to Canada, on a lecture tour.'

180

'Well, take it easy – those lecture tours can be terribly tiring. I know what I'm talking about, I've just returned from one.'

'My secretary tells me you know who murdered Julia Kelburn.'

'Yes, we know, but I'm afraid I can't tell you who it is. The police have clammed up about it.'

'What do you mean – clammed up? I'm not used to these Americanisms.'

'You'll have to get used to them, Doctor, if you're going to Canada. Incidentally, is Mr Cross going with you?'

'Yes, he is.'

'Ah well, he'll put you right, I'm sure.'

'What is it you wanted to ask me, Mr Temple?'

'During your consultations with Julia Kelburn, did she ever mention a friend of hers called Fiona Scott?'

'No, she didn't.'

'You've never heard the name before?'

'No, I haven't. Sorry to disappoint you.'

'Oh, I'm not disappointed. On the contrary, I should have been disappointed if she *had* mentioned it. Goodbye, Dr Benkaray.'

A few days after the visit to the Kelburns' house in the Boltons Temple was having breakfast and listening to the eight o'clock news. The main item was still the big robbery in Bond Street the previous afternoon when thieves had robbed a well-known jewellers in broad daylight. The highly efficient and overworked Metropolitan police appeared baffled by this latest crime, though it bore all the hallmarks of the gang that had given them so much trouble in the past year.

Sir Graham arrived before Steve had put in an appearance. Just as he was finishing his coffee Temple heard Charlie usher him into the sitting-room. He was standing staring morosely out of the window when Temple joined him, with his hands clasped behind his back. To judge by the lines on his face he had not slept the previous night.

'Ah, good morning, Temple,' he said, turning. 'I hope I'm not too early for you, but you sounded quite anxious when you telephoned last night.'

'Good of you to come, Sir Graham. Superintendent—'

'Raine's tied up to his eyes with this Bond Street robbery. We need some lucky break before this afternoon. The Minister has asked me to be at the House of Commons at Question Time.'

'Sit down, Sir Graham. Shall I ask Charlie to bring you a cup of coffee?'

'No, thank you.' Forbes had no time for coffee but he accepted the invitation to take a chair.

'I am more than anxious, I was very worried. I still am,' Temple said. 'Sir Graham, as you know, we've suspected for some time that the murder of Julia Kelburn was linked up with the activities of The Fence.'

'Yes,' Forbes agreed cautiously.

'Well, I've good reason to believe that The Fence has made plans to leave the country – getting out while the going's good. Now, the point is this, Sir Graham. I know who The Fence is, but I haven't sufficient evidence – not real evidence – for you to get a warrant out. On the other hand, once The Fence leaves the country . . .'

'That mustn't be allowed to happen,' Forbes said with quiet emphasis. 'In the present circumstances it would create an impossible situation.'

'Well, how do we prevent it, Sir Graham?'

Forbes knew Temple well enough to read his expression. It told him that his old friend was cooking up one of his complicated plans. 'Have you a suggestion, Temple?'

'Yes, but I'm afraid it's a very unorthodox one. I doubt whether you'll approve of it.'

'I don't mind how unorthodox it is if it's going to help us crack this case.'

Temple hesitated, and Forbes waited patiently for him to continue.

'I had a message from the prison Governor yesterday. Midge Harris has asked if he can see me again. An interview has been arranged for three o'clock this afternoon.'

'Midge Harris?' Forbes repeated the name incredulously. 'He's *asked* to see you! Why on earth? Raine wasn't able to get a word out of the fellow.'

'Ah.' Temple was smiling. 'But Raine never sent him a postcard, Sir Graham!'

Temple's second interview with Midge Harris took place, as before, in the Chaplain's room. Nothing about the prison had changed. The sounds, the smells, the impersonality of the room were just the same. But Midge Harris's manner was completely different. That he was angry was evident from the aggressive thrust of his head and the twist of his mouth. However, he greeted Temple almost like a friend.

'Well, Midge, I came as soon as I could after getting your message.'

'Thanks.' Midge looked over his shoulder, waiting till the warder had closed the door before starting the conversation. 'I had to see you, Mr Temple. For one thing, I wanted to say I'm sorry I didn't believe you last time you were here. You know, when you came out with all that stuff about my girl, Sal.'

'You've heard from her?' Temple proffered the packet of cigarettes which had been untouched since his last visit.

'Yes. I had a postcard. She ain't in the South of France like I told you, she's still in her old job, sweating her guts out. I've been led up the effing garden, and that's a fact.'

'I take it your friends have let you down, then?' Temple asked, holding out his lighter.

Midge put his hand round Temple's to keep the flame steady as he lit his cigarette. It was a symbolic gesture of confidence.

'Let me down! You can say that again! Yes, well, he ain't bloody well goin' to get away with it – not this time, he ain't!'

'I'm glad to hear you say that. After all, apart from the predicament you're in, it's not fair on Sally.'

'You're dead right it ain't fair on Sally! I don't know what's gone wrong. He's always looked after the other boys, always taken care of them . . .'

'Well, he hasn't looked after you, Midge, has he?'

The expletive that escaped from Midge was unprintable and he looked round hurriedly as if afraid that the Chaplain might have materialised behind him. Temple, suppressing a smile of amusement, took a chair and gave Midge a signal to do the same.

'Now, Midge, listen. I want you to tell me about The Fence. I give my word that whatever you tell me about yourself will be treated in the strictest confidence. I'm only interested in The Fence and the Kelburn murder.'

'I didn't have anything to do with any murder!' At the word murder Midge had stiffened. 'You got to believe that, Mr Temple, or you don't get another word out of me!'

'All right, Midge, I believe you,' Temple assured him, placatingly. 'Now tell me how you first got in touch with The Fence.'

Midge drew thoughtfully on his cigarette.

'I'd never heard of him until a few years back when I knocked off a jeweller's and tried to get rid of the stuff through the usual channels. The boys wouldn't hear of it – wouldn't touch the stuff. The Yard had got the heat on just about then – sending scores of their chaps round the pawn shops and places. I tried one or two of the provincial boys but it was the same story – they all said the stuff was too hot.'

'Go on.'

'Well, one day I was in a little caff off the Tottenham Court Road when the man who runs the place said I was wanted on the blower. It was a woman – she didn't give her name but she 'ad a bit of a funny accent. Foreigner, I suppose. Anyway, she said she'd heard I was interested in doing a deal and she told me to go to a pet shop in South Dock Road, Shoreditch. I was to ask for Oscar. Well, I went round to this place – it's next door to a pub called The Greyhound – and spoke to the bloke behind the counter. He was a big, tough-looking chap with a Brummie accent.'

Temple was not taking notes. It would only remind Midge of his interviews with the police. He knew that he would be able to remember the conversation word for word.

'What happened?'

'I showed him a diamond ring I wanted to flog and told him there was plenty more where that came from.'

'Did he buy it?'

'No, 'course he didn't,' Midge said. 'Not right away. They weren't takin' no chances. This Oscar bloke asked me to leave it with him for a couple of days while he had it valued. Well, what'd I got to lose? I couldn't flog it anywhere else. Two days later I got another 'phone call, telling me to take all the stuff to a place called Breakwater House, not far from Brighton.'

Not by a flicker of interest did Temple show that this was the break he had been waiting for. 'And what happened there?'

'A youngish chap let me in – a slick operator type. He collected the stuff off me and took it into the next room. After a minute or two I heard several voices – there seemed to be a bit of an argument going on. I began to wonder what was happening. I mean to say, I was all on my own, and there were three or four of them, as far as I could tell. Still, in the end this young fellow comes back with a real good offer – and what's more it was cash down and no messing about.'

'You didn't see any of the other people?'

'No, I didn't.' Midge laid the remains of his cigarette on the floor and flattened it with the sole of his shoe. 'But the young bloke asked me if I'd be interested in another little job they'd cased out at Ealing – dead easy it was, too. After that, one thing led to another. They kept me pretty busy . . .' A look of happy reminiscence came over Midge's face as he remembered these good times. 'Sometimes with one or two other chaps, sometimes on my own.'

'And you never actually saw The Fence?'

'No, never set eyes on 'im. But he always played fair, Mr Temple – paid a good price and looked after the wife and kids if any of the boys got nabbed. That's what I don't understand about this lark. Why didn't he take care of Sal?'

Midge looked straight at him and Temple would have felt ashamed of his subterfuge if his motive had not been to track down the murderer of Julia Kelburn, Ted Angus and Tony Wyman.

'Yes, well – it's just one of those things,' he said vaguely, and stood up. 'Thank you, Midge, you've been a great help. Take care of yourself.'

Midge took the hint that the interview was ove
that he had done something to level the score bet
and The Fence, he gave Temple a broad grin.

'Well, I won't overeat, if that's what you're worrie

For the second day in succession Steve came into the
room to find Temple almost finishing his breakfast. S
gone to bed the previous night before he came home
had just got to sleep when the sound of his key in the t.
door wakened her. Knowing that he was being as quiet
possible she had kept her eyes closed when he came to bed
Ironically, he had fallen asleep before she did and it was a
long time before she finally drifted away. In the morning she
awoke to find that he had already got up.

She was still sleepy as she came round the table to kiss
him on the top of the head.

'You were out very late last night, Paul. What were you
up to?'

'I tried not to disturb you coming in. I went down to Fleet
Street and had a couple of drinks with Ken Sinclair.'

'That's the second time you've seen Ken within the past week.'

Temple picked up the coffee pot and poured her a cup.
In the hall the 'phone started ringing.

'I've asked him to look up an old friend of ours – Wally Stone.'

'Who's Wally Stone?' Steve asked, without great interest.
She knew she needed her coffee before she could make sense.

'Don't you remember? He used to be one of the best cats
in the business.'

'Cats?' It was too early in the day for Steve to grasp
underworld slang. 'You mean a pantomime cat?'

'No, darling.' When he had finished laughing Temple
became serious. He could hear Charlie dealing with the

phone call. 'Steve, you know the bracelet I bought you
t Christmas – the diamond and ruby one?'

'Yes.'

'I'd like to borrow it for a couple of days. I think the
clasp needs attention.'

'It doesn't. The clasp's perfectly all right.'

'I don't think so, Steve. I noticed it the other evening when
we went to the Kelburns. It needs looking at. It'll only take
a day or two.'

Steve was still looking puzzled when Charlie brought the
telephone in. 'Sir Graham Forbes for you, sir,' he said, as he
plugged it into the socket.

With a slightly apprehensive look at Steve, Temple took
the instrument. 'Temple here. Good morning, Sir Graham.'

'Temple, we've done what you wanted.' Forbes's resonant
voice was clearly audible from Steve's place across the table.
'We've included the ruby and diamond bracelet in the list of
stolen property. A description has been sent out to all stations,
as well as to jewellers, pawnbrokers and, of course, the Press.'

'Thank you, Sir Graham,' Temple said hurriedly, showing
no desire to prolong the conversation. But Sir Graham too
was in a hurry and rang off with an abrupt, 'Right! Goodbye.'

Steve was staring at Paul over the top of her cup. The
hot, strong coffee had put life in her.

'Paul, did he say a ruby and diamond bracelet?'

'Yes, I believe he did.'

'But you just asked me to—'

'Just one of those unhappy coincidences, darling.'

The Greyhound in Shoreditch was easy to find. Under new
ownership it had been smartened up with a fresh coat of paint
and bore the usual signs – Free House, Real Ale and The Inn

Place for Good Grub. The same could not be said for the pet shop next door to it. The paint was peeling, the windows needed cleaning and the stock on display in them had been there for a long time. Though the owner had forgotten to reverse the Closed sign the door opened when Temple turned the handle. He found himself in a gloomy shop with tins of dog and cat food round the wall, bags of fodder on the floor, a festoon of dog leads hanging from a coat-hook. A couple of white rabbits peered out from behind the bars of a tiny cage and a bird with brilliant plumage squawked a greeting – or a warning – from a bird-cage hung from the ceiling.

The man behind the counter was not all that pleased to see a customer come in. He was a burly fellow with an over-developed paunch and flabby cheeks. He might have been an all-in wrestler gone to seed. He ran suspicious eyes over Temple's clothes and features and decided that he represented a type which he spurned.

'What can I do for you?' he asked, or rather demanded. As Midge had said, the accent was Birmingham.

'You've got a dog collar in the window. It's marked ten pounds fifty.'

'That's right.' Oscar's eyes dropped to Temple's well-polished shoes.

'Is it leather?'

'Yes, 'course it's leather – genuine leather.'

'Do you think I could have a look at it?'

'I've got one here.' Oscar made no attempt to move. 'It's a different colour, but it's just the same.' He opened a drawer and produced a bright scarlet dog collar. 'Very good value for ten fifty. Is it the right size?'

'Yes, it is.' Temple took the collar and examined it cursorily. 'But it's not quite the same as the one in the window, is it?'

189

'It's exactly the same.' Behind him the tropical bird squawked a protest. 'That's leather, that is – genuine leather.' Oscar seized the collar and angrily flexed it.

'I'll take it.'

Oscar reacted almost with resentment, cheated of a good, abrasive row. 'Okay,' he said, and began to put the collar in a bag.

Temple put ten pounds and a fifty-pence piece on the counter. 'Are you Oscar?'

'Yes. What of it?'

'I think you know a friend of mine – Midge Harris?'

'Don't know anyone called Harris.' Oscar kept his eyes down.

'A small, rather scruffy little man with a red . . .'

'Don't know anyone called Harris,' Oscar repeated, more vehemently.

'No?' Temple had one hand in his jacket pocket. 'I'm sorry about that. I thought you might be able to tell me what this was worth.' He brought out his hand and put Steve's ruby and diamond necklace on the counter.

Oscar reeled back as if he had been struck. 'Strewth! Where did you get that from?'

'I'll give you one guess.'

'That's from the Bond Street job!'

'That's right.'

Oscar glanced instinctively at the door, then contemplated Temple with new eyes.

'Have you got the rest of the stuff, then?' he asked, with almost awed respect.

'Yes.'

'Where?'

'Don't be silly.' Temple laughed. 'Do you think I'm going to tell you that?'

'Why did you come here?' Realisation was dawning on Oscar. 'You didn't want a dog collar—'

'Of course I didn't. I'm in a spot, I've got to get rid of this stuff, it's red hot. Look, if you're prepared to help me I'll cut you in . . .'

'Listen, pal – don't get me wrong. I'm not The Fence, I'm just the go-between. How do I know this bracelet is genuine, anyway?'

'Doesn't it look genuine?'

'Oh, yes, it looks genuine.' Oscar's wheezy chuckle came from the depths of his belly. 'But so does the dog collar.'

'Well, what do I do – ditch the stuff? I've got God knows how much stuff tucked away in . . .' Temple picked up the bracelet, angry and frustrated. 'Okay, if you're not interested . . .'

'No, wait a minute!' Oscar put a hand over Temple's, holding it down. 'He'll have to see this bracelet, you know – he'll have to examine it.'

'That's all right by me. I'll leave the bracelet with you. How long will it take him to make up his mind?'

Oscar picked the bracelet up. From the drawer he took a jeweller's magnifying glass and fitted it into one eye. He peered at the bracelet from a range of three inches.

'About forty-eight hours. Come back on Thursday morning.'

CHAPTER VIII

The Visitor

Though he'd had the lucky break he needed, though he knew who The Fence was, though he had a plan to secure conclusive evidence Paul Temple could do nothing further without the help of Wally Stone. And Wally Stone was taking his time. While Forbes was kept busy by the repercussions of the Bond Street burglary and Raine persevered with the laborious procedures of a multiple murder investigation, Temple occupied himself by typing out the final version of his latest book.

He had done about ten thousand words – several days' work – before his enforced period of waiting ended. He had been over to the London Library one morning to verify some dates and locations. When he arrived home a little after midday Steve informed him that 'his friend' had turned up and was waiting for him in the sitting-room.

'What friend?'

'You know, the one who's not a pantomime cat.'

'Oh, Wally Stone! How long has he been here?'

'About ten minutes. We had a nice little chat. Is he a clergyman, Paul?'

Temple laughed. 'Not exactly, darling.'

Wally Stone did indeed look more like a pillar of the church than a retired cat burglar. His dark suit was well-cut, his shoes hand-tooled, his hands carefully manicured. His features had the aesthetic quality of a philosopher and his speech was that of an old-fashioned schoolmaster.

'Good afternoon, Mr Stone. Sorry to have kept you waiting.'

Wally moved away from the mantelpiece, where he had been admiring a Faberge box.

'Good afternoon, Mr Temple. Mr Sinclair told me that you were anxious to see me and as I just happened to be in town for the day . . .'

'Yes, that's right. Would you care for a glass of sherry?'

Wally nodded graciously. 'Thank you, Mr Temple, that would be very agreeable.' Temple went to the drinks cabinet to pour two glasses. 'What a delightful room. I've been admiring your fireplace.'

'Yes, it is rather pleasant, isn't it?'

When handed his glass Wally held it to the light, inspecting its colour before taking an appreciative sip.

'Mr Stone,' Temple began, as the two men sat down, 'I'm sure you'd prefer that I didn't beat about the bush, and came straight to the point. I'm working with the police on an important case – unfortunately our investigations are held up because we've failed to secure a vital piece of evidence.'

'Yes?' said Wally quietly, his interest sharpening.

'Well, it seems that the only way for us to get this evidence is for someone to break into a certain house and – search for it.'

'I see. And I take it, that's why I'm here?'

'Yes. And there is a certain urgency about this.'

'And what is this piece of evidence, exactly?'

'It's a diamond and ruby bracelet. It belongs to my wife.'

'Your wife?' Wally was not easily taken aback, but his thick black eyebrows shot up in surprise. 'Then the bracelet was stolen from you?'

'Don't worry too much about the finer details of this assignment, Wally,' Temple said smiling. He handed Wally a card. 'Here's the address. If you don't find the bracelet, give me a ring. If you do – come straight back here.'

Wally stared at the card, memorising the address, then handed it back. 'And what if anything goes wrong?'

'Nothing must go wrong. However, if you do get into trouble, don't worry, I'll get you out of it.'

'Very well, Mr Temple. I'll be pleased to deal with this little assignment for you.'

'You haven't asked me what the job's worth.'

Wally pondered for a moment. He was reluctant to discuss the commercial aspect of the matter but realised that some agreement should be made.

'Well, what is it worth? Ten per cent of the value of the bracelet?'

Temple laughed at this very modest claim. 'We'll talk about that later.'

'Anyway, it isn't so much the money, Mr Temple, it's the nostalgia that appeals to me. It'll be just like old times. Life's so tedious since I retired . . .'

'Yes, well, don't forget,' Temple warned, 'We're *only* interested in the bracelet.' He didn't want Wally to become over-enthusiastic.

During lunch Temple parried Steve's questions about Wally. She could tell that they were cooking up some plot together and her natural curiosity was aroused. Charlie had brought the coffee into the sitting-room when the telephone rang.

Sir Graham Forbes was ringing from Scotland Yard and his news was disturbing.

'We've had a message through from Westerton, Temple. You know that woman who worked for Dr Benkaray?'

'Mrs Fletcher, yes.'

'She has a son—'

'That's right – Bill. He runs the garage.'

'He was knocked down by a car early this morning. He's in Westerton Hospital.'

'Is he badly hurt?'

'Yes, I'm afraid he is. We don't know what happened, exactly. The car didn't stop. But the point is, Temple, the boy's asking for his mother and we just don't know where she is. She's not at the garage.'

'That doesn't surprise me. When Steve saw her the other morning she said she was leaving for Australia.'

'She hasn't been in touch with either of you since then?'

'No. For all I know she's left already.'

'She hasn't. Raine has checked with the airlines. She's got a BA booking for tonight. Flight BA 109 to Melbourne. We'll just have to wait till then.'

'What time does it leave?'

'The take-off is scheduled for nine fifteen. She'll be checking in by eight fifteen.'

'Sir Graham—'

'Yes?'

'I've got a suggestion to make.'

'What is it?'

'Don't send Raine to the airport. Let Steve deal with Mrs Fletcher.'

*

Heathrow Airport, and especially Terminal 3, brought back memories of that night when she had come here to meet Temple. Steve steeled herself as she drove into the multi-storey car park, up the giddily twisting spiral ramp to the fourth level where she at last found space. She locked the car and made a careful note of its position. Mrs Fletcher would have to check in before 8.15, but it was likely that she would leave herself a wider margin than that and Steve did not want to take any chances. It was only 7.30 when she took the lift down to ground level.

The departure hall was thronged with a milling crowd of men, women and children of every nationality. Most of them were suffering from pre-flight nerves, intent on their own problems. Jostled and shoved, she had to push her way through to the British Airways desk. A helpful, but somewhat remote girl in her blue and white uniform consented to find out if Mrs Fletcher had checked in yet. Steve was grateful for modern computerisation when the information came back within seconds. Mrs Fletcher had already registered her baggage but there was no way of telling whether she had yet passed through Emigration into the Departure Lounge. If she had, Steve would have lost her.

'I can put out a call for her on the public address system,' the BA girl suggested.

Steve hesitated. The sound of her name booming out through the terminal could send Mrs Fletcher scuttling for refuge in the Departure Lounge.

She said: 'I'll see if I can find her and if I can't I'll come back.'

The girl nodded and turned her attention to the next passenger.

Struggling through the crowd Steve checked the cafeteria, the shops, the bank, and even the ladies' lavatories. But there was no sign of a middle-aged English woman with rosy cheeks and a matronly bosom. Steve climbed the stairs to the balcony, which ran round the main hall. From here she could look down on the people below and also watch the entrance to the Departure Lounge. Her luck was in. On the opposite side, seated on one of the upholstered benches, was a lone woman. Her head was bent as she rummaged in her flight bag, but Steve recognised the hat. It was the one Mrs Fletcher had worn when she came to visit the flat. She seemed reluctant to take the final decisive step of passing through Emigration which would separate her from England, her garage, and Bill.

Steve sauntered casually round the balcony, hoping she would not look up.

'Good evening, Mrs Fletcher,' she said quietly.

Mrs Fletcher started and her head jerked up. 'Why – It's Mrs Temple!'

'That's right.' Steve sat down beside her. 'I've been looking for you everywhere, Mrs Fletcher.'

Mrs Fletcher was suspicious and faintly hostile. 'What is it you want?'

Steve's reply was drowned by the loudspeakers making yet another announcement.

'Passengers on Flight 109 to Melbourne should proceed to the Departure Lounge now. Boarding will commence in thirty minutes.'

'That's my flight!' Mrs Fletcher grabbed her flight bag. 'I must go . . .'

Steve put out a restraining hand. 'Wait a minute, Mrs Fletcher! I'm afraid I've got some bad news for you.'

'This is a trick! I know what you're up to! It's a trick to try and stop me from . . .'

'Bill's had a serious accident. He's in Westerton Hospital.'

Steve had intended to break the news more gently but Mrs Fletcher's panic and suspicion had forced her to be brutally open. The woman's chin dropped.

'I don't believe you!'

'It's true, I assure you.'

'What – what happened?'

'He was knocked down by a car early this morning. The car didn't stop. Whether it was an accident or not we don't know.'

'How bad is he?'

'Well, he's on the danger list. He wants to see you, Mrs Fletcher. He keeps asking for you.'

Mrs Fletcher stared at Steve, her lips trembling as she fought with conflicting emotions. 'If this isn't true – if this is some kind of a plot to keep me from leaving . . .'

'Look, Mrs Fletcher,' Steve burst out with genuine anger and frustration, 'if you want to catch that plane, catch it! I'm not stopping you! I promised my husband I'd see you and tell you what had happened. It's up to you whether you believe me or not!'

Mrs Fletcher shook her head. She looked towards the entrance to the Departure Lounge and then back at Steve.

'You say he's in Westerton Hospital?'

'Yes. In the Casualty Ward. You can ring the hospital if you like. Westerton 824.'

'No . . . No, I believe you. This accident, Mrs Temple. You say the car didn't stop?'

'That's right.'

'I ought to have realised something like this would happen,' Mrs Fletcher said, and then with sudden venom, 'The bastard!'

Steve knew she had won her confidence.

'I've got my car outside. I'll run you straight down to Westerton.'

'Thank you, Mrs Temple, but what about my baggage? It's already registered and my ticket's been—'

Steve picked up the flight bag and took Mrs Fletcher's arm.

'Don't worry, my husband will take care of that for you. Come along, Mrs Fletcher. Stay close to me.'

Charlie had gone to bed at eleven o'clock and, as usual, had immediately fallen asleep. The telephone ringing had disturbed him briefly, but it had been answered almost at once. Then, a few hours later he woke again with a sense that something was wrong. He could not identify the sound that had alerted him; it could have been a door closing. He switched on the light and peered at his alarm clock. It was two o'clock, give or take a few minutes. He got up, put on a dressing-gown – one of Mr Temple's discarded garments – over his pyjamas and went out to the hall. From the study he could hear the steady tap of the typewriter. Impelled by his insatiable curiosity, he barged in without knocking and stopped, pretending to be surprised.

'Oh, sorry, Mr Temple . . .'

Temple was sitting in front of the typewriter on his desk, which was covered with papers. He swivelled round in his chair.

'Anything wrong, Charlie?'

'No, sir, but I heard a noise. I didn't know you were in here.'

'Sorry if I disturbed you,' Temple said drily.

'No, that's all right, Mr Temple. It's two o'clock in the morning, you know.'

'Yes, I know.'

'Is Mrs Temple still out?'

'Yes, she's still out.' Temple smiled at Charlie's disapproving shake of the head. 'It's all right, Charlie, she's not on the tiles, if that's what you're thinking. I know where she is. She had to go down to Westerton.'

'Oh, I see.' Charlie brightened. 'Well, would you like me to get some coffee, Mr Temple, while you're waiting for her?'

'No, I'm all right. Just leave me, Charlie, I want to get on with . . .' He stopped at the sound of the front door opening and closing. 'Is that the front door?'

'Yes, it must be Mrs Temple!' No father, hearing his teenage daughter returning after an evening date, could have looked more relieved than Charlie.

'Paul!'

'I'm in the study, darling.'

Steve came in, thrusting the car keys into her handbag. She was tired, but triumphant. 'Paul, you shouldn't have waited up. Or you, Charlie!'

'Good evening—' Charlie cleared his throat. 'I mean – morning, Mrs Temple.'

'Charlie,' Temple said, 'I think we'll take you up on that offer of some coffee.'

'Yes, that's a wonderful idea!' Steve took off her coat and threw it over the back of a chair.

'Okay. Right away, Mrs Temple!' Charlie hurried into the kitchen.

'Well, how did you get on, Steve?'

Temple exchanged his desk chair for one of the leather armchairs. Steve took the other, stretching her arms and legs.

'It all went according to plan. Mrs Fletcher was a bit suspicious at first, but eventually she realised I was telling the truth.'

'And what about Bill?'

'He's had the operation and he's still very ill, but they think he'll pull through. Mrs Fletcher was so relieved when she heard he'd got over the operation that she agreed to do everything you wanted. She's staying the night at the hospital. I said we'd drive down there tomorrow.'

'Good.'

'She's very bitter about Dr Benkaray, Paul. You know, I'm sure Mrs Fletcher isn't really a crook – at least, not a professional one.'

'I never thought she was. And that's the danger, Steve. The other people realise that, too. They know she's the weakest link in the chain. But tell me, what else did she say?'

'She explained about the coat that was found in my car with the name Margo in it. It appears that just about then Mrs Fletcher discovered the gang had extended its activities and were going in for drug smuggling.'

'And she disapproved?'

'She certainly did! Particularly when she discovered that she'd been distributing drugs without realising it. You see, from time to time they asked her to take certain coats down to Brighton. The coats were handed over to Margo, the fortune teller, who distributed the drugs.'

'The drugs were concealed in the coats, then?'

'Yes. That explains why they were so heavy. Anyway, when they gave Mrs Fletcher another coat to deliver she decided she wouldn't and that she'd tell them so. Larry Cross was just leaving for Heathrow when she tackled him about it. The argument continued all the way to the airport. Finally, Cross lost his temper, pushed her to one side, and concentrated on the matter in hand . . .'

'Which was the kidnapping of you?'

'Yes. Mrs Fletcher was furious, and she tossed the coat into my car and caught the Underground back to town. She thought Cross would return to the car and pick up the coat.'

'I see. Did she let you into any more of her secrets?'

'She admitted that she tipped us off about the fortune teller, then tricked the woman into telling us about Breakwater House. You know, Paul, I can't help but think that we owe a great deal to . . . Are you expecting anyone?'

A long peal on the doorbell had sounded very loud at this hour of the night.

'Yes,' said Temple calmly. 'Wally Stone. He 'phoned a couple of hours ago.'

Wally was as gracious as ever when a scandalised Charlie showed him in. He was wearing the same sober suit as on the previous occasion. The right jacket pocket was bulging.

'Sorry I could not be here sooner, Mr Temple,' he said, when he had greeted Steve with his usual courtesy. 'But I did not like to come in my working clothes.'

'You haven't wasted any time, Wally.'

'No,' Wally agreed modestly. 'However, there was no point in delaying. Mealtimes are often the most favourable for my work. When people are at dinner they and their servants are usually fully occupied.'

'Charlie,' Temple told his own mystified servant, 'bring in the coffee as soon as it's ready. You'll join us in some coffee, Wally?'

'Delighted, Mr Temple. Can't think of anything I'd like better – except perhaps a whisky and soda.'

'Yes, of course. Bring in the decanter, Charlie.'

'Yes, sir.' Charlie dragged his eyes from Wally and went off to obey the order.

'Well, how did it go?'

'I had to open a safe, Mr Temple. Very neat little job it was too, concealed in an alcove just behind the fireplace. Took a bit of finding.'

'Was it much trouble to open?'

'Tiresome, you know,' Wally's gesture was deprecating, 'a little tiresome.'

'And what was inside?'

'Loads of stuff. My goodness, yes. Had a bit of a job sorting out what I'd come for. Lucky you gave me a good description.' Wally put a hand in his jacket pocket. 'There we are – that's the bracelet, isn't it, Mr Temple?'

'Yes,' said Temple, taking it. 'That's the one.'

Steve took a step forward. 'But that's my bracelet, Paul!'

'Yes, I know, darling.'

'But how on earth . . .'

'I left your bracelet with a man called Oscar. He thought it was stolen property. He's a go-between, works for The Fence.'

'Then how did Mr Stone get hold of it?'

'He's just told you, he stole it – from a house in London. The Fence's house.'

Steve turned to Wally and nodded slowly with comprehension. Wally smiled modestly.

'I see,' she said. '*That* sort of cat.'

Mrs Fletcher did not get much sleep that night. It had been nearly midnight when Mrs Temple delivered her at the hospital. A compassionate Matron had allowed her to see Bill for a few minutes. He was still on the danger list, but conscious. Though unable to talk, he opened his eyes and saw who it was. He managed a faint smile and then relaxed into a deep sleep. Mrs Fletcher was given a bed in a room that was available for such emergencies and

managed to snatch a few hours' sleep. In the morning the
nurses told her that they were very pleased with Bill and
now believed that he would pull through. Her arrival had
been the turning-point. He was still in a deep natural sleep
and they advised her not to disturb him until 'Doctor' had
paid his visit.

Mrs Fletcher was not an ungrateful woman and she
did not forget the promise she had made to Steve. There
was a pay 'phone on the ground floor of the hospital and
as soon as she'd had some breakfast she went into it and
dialled a number.

As she had expected it was Larry Cross who answered,
ill-tempered as always.

'Mr Cross, this is Mrs Fletcher.'

'Fletcher? I thought you'd gone abroad!'

'I – I changed my mind.'

'Well, if you take my tip you'll change it again and get
the blazes out of here!'

'I want to see Dr Benkaray . . .'

'What do you want to see her for?'

Mrs Fletcher had always been bullied by Cross and up
till now had knuckled under. But the thought of Bill lying
injured on the floor above gave her courage. 'I'll tell that
to the doctor.'

'She's extremely busy this morning, she can't see anybody.'

'I've got to see her, I tell you. It's important.'

The urgency of her voice got through to Cross. 'What's
this all about, Fletcher?'

'It's about some letters I have, and some tape recordings.
Dr Benkaray knows all about them. They're in a deed box at
the bank. Tell the doctor if she'll meet me I'm now prepared
to do a deal.'

Cross did not reply for a long time and Mrs Fletcher had to put another coin in the slot.

'All right. Come to the house this morning – about eleven o' clock. I'll tell the doctor to expect you.'

'No, I can't do that.'

'Why not? It's broad daylight.'

'It was broad daylight when Ted Angus turned up, wasn't it? I'm at the hospital at Westerton, I think you know why. I'll meet you both in the visitors' car park outside the hospital in about an hour. We can talk in your car.'

She hung up before he could object. She stayed where she was till her trembling had subsided, then pushed the door open to escape from the booth.

In fact, it was an hour and twenty minutes before she went out to the visitors' car park. Matron had asked her to come and see the doctor who was in charge of Bill's case and they had stayed talking at his bedside for some time.

She saw with some satisfaction that they were still there waiting for her in Dr Benkaray's Peugeot. She had no alternative but to sit in the front seat beside Dr Benkaray with Larry Cross in the seat behind her. It was hard to break out of the old submissive mood but she had drawn confidence from the thought that they were both here at her command.

When Dr Benkaray heard about the letters and tape recordings she tried her usual tactics.

'Now, pull yourself together, Mrs Fletcher, and let's try to be sensible.'

'If I'd really known what was going on, Dr Benkaray, I'd never have let you talk me into it. For weeks and weeks I've been trying to get away.'

'You're too involved, Mrs Fletcher. You've got to take your chance with the rest of us. You didn't object to the money.'

'I would have if I'd known what it was all about!'

'Don't be a hypocrite – you knew, all right!'

She could smell Larry Cross's breath. He was leaning forward, his face right behind her.

'I kept telling you that Bill knew nothing about all this – yet you ran him down like that, in cold blood!'

'I assure you we know nothing about that accident, nothing whatever,' Dr Benkaray said. 'Now what's all this about letters and tape recordings? You mentioned this to me once before. What are they, exactly?'

'You know what they are! They're photostat copies of letters you received and tape recordings of telephone conversations. I took them while I was working for you.'

'Why, you interfering . . .' Larry exploded. She felt her seat shake as he thumped the headrest with his fist.

'Shut up, Larry!' Dr Benkaray snapped.

'When I found out what was going on I had to protect myself. Especially after Ted Angus was murdered. I – I always had a soft spot for Ted.'

'And what exactly did you plan to do with these letters?'

'I was going to hand them over to the police, if there was ever any attempt on my life – or Bill's.'

'I assure you no one is going to make any attempt on your life.'

'The trouble is I can't believe you any more. Look what happened to my son.'

'Mrs Fletcher, will you please listen to me!' Dr Benkaray was obviously losing patience. 'You must realise that you can't leave that box at the bank without taking some precautions. What's to prevent your son opening it at any time? Don't you see, it would get a lot of people into serious trouble – yourself included. If you value your son's life you'd better hand the contents of that deed box over straight away.'

Instead of intimidating Mrs Fletcher, the threat against Bill emboldened her. 'I'm prepared to hand it over – but only to The Fence in person.'

'But you don't know The Fence, you've never met him. So why should . . .'

'I know that, but I'm not prepared to hand it over to anyone else – and I'm only prepared to hand it over to him on one condition. He's got to give an assurance – a definite assurance – that he'll leave Bill alone in the future.'

'I think he'll agree to that, Mrs Fletcher,' said Dr Benkaray, apparently prepared to accept these terms. 'Get the box from the bank today – and take it to your garage. You'll have a visitor this evening – at eleven o'clock.'

'I hope I did the right thing, Mr Temple.'

'You certainly did, Mrs Fletcher, and I'm very grateful to you.'

'Well, I felt it was the least I could do. I do apologise for my behaviour to Mrs Temple last night. When I think that if it wasn't for her—'

Temple and Steve had reached Westerton at midday and driven straight to the hospital. They had found Mrs Fletcher enjoying the morning sunshine in a garden at the back of the building. It was under the windows of the ward where Bill's bed was screened off and the Ward Sister had promised to call her if he woke and asked for her. Having enquired first about her son, they had to listen to a long report on his condition and exactly what the doctor had said before she got round to her conversation with Larry Cross and Dr Benkaray. She had a remarkably good memory and was able to give it to them verbatim, with plenty of 'says she' and 'says I'.

'You've been very frank about the whole affair,' Temple congratulated her. 'But now, I'm afraid I've got to ask you to do something else.'

'I'll do anything – anything you ask, Mr Temple,' she told him, exchanging a woman's glance with Steve.

'I'd like you to go through with this, Mrs Fletcher. I'd like you to get the deed box from the bank and take it to the garage. I'd like you to be there tonight – when The Fence arrives.'

Mrs Fletcher started to shake her head. She had screwed up the courage to face Dr Benkaray but the thought of meeting the anonymous and shadowy figure known as The Fence terrified her. Then the drone of an airliner climbing from Gatwick reminded her that but for the Temples, she would be nearly in Australia by now.

'All right. If that's what you want, I'll be there.'

'Thank you, Mrs Fletcher,' Temple said seriously. 'Now this is what I want you to do. Listen carefully . . .'

Darkness had fallen at about a quarter to nine. By half past ten the unmarked police car was parked between the privet hedges of the drive to a house opposite Fletcher's Garage. The occupants of the house had been asked to draw their curtains, leave the lights on and behave as if nothing was happening. Like Temple's it was a Rover with the 3.5 litre engine, but this one had been boosted with a turbo charger to give it extra performance. In it were seated four men. Superintendent Raine was in the passenger seat beside his own driver, PC Newton. In the back sat Sir Graham Forbes and Temple.

As the operation to trap The Fence had been planned by Raine, with the co-operation of the Kent Constabulary, Temple had to accept the role of observer. Nevertheless he had taken the precaution of making a thorough reconnaissance of the garage that afternoon, noting all possible approaches and exits. Mrs Fletcher's and Bill's house was a detached building beside the garage, separated from it by an open passage. A door in the side of the house was opposite the side door of the garage. Behind both vehicles was a big yard, used for the breakdown lorry, a few second-hand cars for sale, and the cars of customers awaiting collection or repair. The repair shop extended into this yard from behind the showroom and was approached by a gate near the self-service area where Steve had waited so patiently. He knew that two other police cars were poised ready to close in on a radio signal from Raine and that four more would move into the area when it was confirmed that Mrs Fletcher's 'visitor' had arrived.

At seven minutes to eleven one of those unexpected hitches occurred. A motorist, running out of petrol, pulled into the forecourt of the garage, ignoring the Closed sign, and the darkened office. As he got out it was obvious that he intended to knock up the garage owner.

'Go and sort him out, Newton,' Raine told his driver.

With great presence of mind Newton took his emergency can of petrol out of the boot and sauntered across the road.

'In trouble?' they heard him call out.

The motorist stopped a few yards short of Mrs Fletcher's porch and came back, a little unsteadily, to his car. After a brief conversation they saw Newton unscrew the filler cap and dump half a gallon of petrol into the tank. With profuse thanks to the uniformed Samaritan, the motorist drove away.

It was three minutes to eleven when Newton got back into the car. Raine exhaled his breath.

'That took ten years off my life,' he said.

'There's a car coming down the High Street very slowly.' Forbes was craning his neck to see over the low hedge. 'This could be our man.'

There was no more conversation as they all watched the car slow down. The driver doused his headlights as he turned in, using only sidelights as he drew up on the far side of the pumps. They saw the white lights at the rear come on as he engaged reverse. Then he reversed neatly between two cars, bearing FOR SALE notices, parked beside the self-service area. They saw him climb out, a shadowy outline, and walk quickly towards Mrs Fletcher's front door. He was wearing a slouch hat and had his overcoat collar turned up. It was impossible to see his face. Once at the porch he turned round and Raine commanded: 'Heads down!'

All four men dropped their heads so that the pale blobs of their faces would not be visible. When they looked up again the figure had vanished.

'Is he inside?'

'Must be,' Raine said. 'She would have been waiting to open the door the moment he rang.'

Temple checked his watch. The luminous dial showed him that it was two minutes past eleven.

'How long are you going to give him?'

'Four minutes, five at the most,' Raine said, and picked up his mike.

Temple watched the sweep hand of his watch complete two circuits. To the west of the village a train rumbled past. A lad on a scooter buzzed down the village street, probably a customer from The Red Hart.

'I'll never forgive myself if anything happens to Mrs Fletcher,' Temple murmured to Forbes. 'I'm relying on you to see that she's let down lightly, Sir Graham.'

'Don't worry, Temple. I'll have a talk with the Public Prosecutor. I think Midge Harris deserves a break too.'

'Damn!' It was Raine. 'He's out already. He must have come out of the side door.'

'I think he's spotted us,' Forbes said.

Temple could see the overcoated man now. He was standing just inside the passageway between the garage and the house. He was staring straight at the police car.

'Lights!' said Raine into his mike.

Instantly the forecourt, garage and house were floodlit as the two police cars, which had crept to within fifty yards of the garage from opposite directions, switched on their main beams.

The dark figure turned its head first to left, then to right. Temple could now see that he had a small deed box under one arm. The 'visitor' summed the situation up in one second. He turned his back and disappeared into the passageway.

'He's making for the rear,' Raine said. 'It's all right. I've got two cars on the roads at the back. He won't get—'

But Temple was already out of the car. As he raced across the road, silhouetted by the headlights, the two police cars were moving in. He headed, not for the passageway, but for the self-service area. His route took him past the 'visitor's' car and then he was through the door that led into the yard at the back. In here it was pitch dark and he had been dazzled by the headlights. But the other man had the same disadvantage and he was also handicapped by not knowing the lie of the land as Temple did.

Still running, Temple weaved his way between the parked vehicles, making for the door that led to the fields, with the intention of cutting the man off. Then his quarry made a mistake. The smack of a bullet on the breakdown lorry behind Temple was accompanied by the report of a heavy automatic. He had missed and given his position away. Temple knew now that he was near the door to the fields. When he heard it creak on rusty hinges he gambled that his man had gone through. Ten seconds later he was through himself, flattening his body against the wall on the other side. His eyes had grown accustomed to the darkness now and fifty yards ahead he saw the fugitive, running towards the dark line of a hedge.

'Temple!' he heard Forbes bellowing somewhere behind him. 'Where are you?'

He did not answer, saving his breath for a sprint. The 'visitor' turned round as he heard Temple pounding behind him. He halted and squandered five seconds getting off a shot. The bullet whizzed wide of its target. Then he peeled off the overcoat, dropped the deed box and bolted like a terrified horse. But he had lost momentum. In twenty more paces Temple was up with him. He brought him down with a flying Rugby tackle.

Temple felt the man twist under him as he tried to get his gun hand free. The face was turned upwards, offering him a target he could not resist.

'That's for Julia!' he grunted, as his fist connected with Langdon's jaw. 'And that's for Tony—'

But Langdon had already slumped, his bloodied face kissing the grass. As Temple straightened up, he was lit by the lights of a car that came wallowing and bumping across the field.

'Temple, are you all right?'

It was Raine's voice. Still seeing red, Temple heard the car skid to a halt just short of him. The door was flung open. 'You know,' he gasped, 'I'm getting a little old for this sort of thing.'

'Oh, I wouldn't say that,' Raine commented drily. He turned Langdon's head so that his face was illuminated by the headlights. 'You've made a mess of Mr Langdon.'

Temple studied his handiwork with a mixture of pride and shame. 'By Timothy! I have, haven't I?'

The *Wyoming*, a sister ship of the *Wisconsin*, was due to sail from Southampton at midday. The Kelburns had one of the Verandah Cabins on A Deck. It was a self-contained luxury suite with its own bathroom, telephone, fridge and radio. Close-carpeted from wall to wall, its special feature was the verandah, sumptuously furnished as a sitting-room, and full-length picture windows giving a panoramic view of the sea. This accommodation had set George Kelburn back several thousand pounds for the trip to Jamaica, but it still did not satisfy Laura, who was grumpily hanging her dresses up in the fitted wardrobes.

At the moment the verandah windows commanded a view not of the sea but of the Queen Elizabeth II Terminal and the docks beyond. The liner was still connected to land by the gangway, though all the passengers had been aboard for some time. The public address system had already issued the last warning for all visitors to go ashore.

'We should be sailing in about fifteen minutes,' George Kelburn said. He had not touched his own baggage, knowing that the steward would unpack and put his clothes away. He was wearing a new lightweight suit in anticipation of the warmer climes ahead.

'Don't you want to go on deck?' Laura said, making it clear that she would prefer to have the suite to herself so that she could get things organised the way she wanted them.

'Not particularly,' he said. He went over to the windows and stood looking down on the quayside below.

'This is a change for you, George, isn't it?' she said in her carping voice. 'No telephone to answer, nobody to boss about, no last-minute instructions, none of your . . . What are you staring at?'

He did not answer.

'I asked you what you were staring at.'

'I was just – looking out of the window, that's all.'

He turned back and to her surprise his expression was affectionate.

'Laura, this is supposed to be a pleasure cruise. Let's try not to get on each other's nerves.'

'There aren't enough hangers for my dresses,' she grumbled, rejecting his attempt to be conciliatory.

'All right. Ring for the steward. Or better still, go and have a word with the Purser. Let the poor devil know what he's in for.'

She ignored that remark, went into the bathroom and turned the key. George Kelburn changed his mind about unpacking. He opened the smallest of his suitcases, found his wallet of toilet accessories and extracted a small medicine bottle with two capsules in it. He closed his fist over them as Laura emerged from the bathroom.

'Well, when I see the Purser I'm going to complain about this bathroom. It's absurdly small.'

'Very well,' George said wearily. 'You do that.'

At the door she paused. 'Don't leave the cabin. I want you here when I come back.'

He smiled. 'That you can depend on, Laura.'

When she had closed the door George went to the bedside table where a drinking tumbler had been placed over a carafe of iced water. Thoughtfully, he took the tumbler off, poured a quarter of a glass of water and waited. He seemed to be listening. When there came a knock on the door, he tipped the capsules into his mouth, put the glass to his lips and swallowed. Then he put the glass down, turned to the door and called: 'Come in.'

'Good afternoon, Kelburn,' said Paul Temple, entering and closing the door behind him. 'I thought you weren't taking your trip until the end of the month?'

Temple was disappointed at the lack of reaction from the man at his unexpected appearance.

'I changed my mind.'

'A sudden decision?'

'Yes – a sudden decision. Where are the police? I saw them on the quay . . .'

'They're talking to your wife.'

Kelburn nodded. He seemed to be taking all this as the most natural thing in the world. 'You picked up Langdon, I suppose?'

'We did. Also Dr Benkaray and Larry Cross.'

Temple had not come far into the room. He knew that something was wrong. Kelburn's behaviour and speech were not in character.

'Langdon talked?' Kelburn asked, without great interest.

'He had to, otherwise the police might have believed he was The Fence – instead of you. He was most anxious that they shouldn't think that, Mr Kelburn. Still, we've got enough evidence against you without Langdon.'

'You mean Mrs Fletcher and the deed box?'

216

'Yes, and the fact that my wife's bracelet turned up at your house.'

'Your wife's . . .' At last Kelburn showed some interest. 'So that was it? You were the burglar?'

'By proxy. You know, you've worried me, Kelburn. I should have been on to you earlier – I should have realised what Tony Wyman meant when he said "Kelburn – The Fence". He wasn't warning you against the electrified fence – he was warning me against you, Kelburn.'

'That young man overreached himself.'

'I don't think you can criticise him on that account.'

'He thought he knew all the answers, Temple – just like you do.' Kelburn suddenly lost balance. He put a hand on the back of a chair to steady himself. His eyes had widened. 'But . . . you don't . . . know . . .' His body sagged. He had to support himself on both hands to remain upright.

'What is it, Kelburn?' Temple started towards him.

Kelburn twisted his head round, his mouth distorted by a grimace.

'I – I took something just before – you came in.' Kelburn gasped and put a hand to his throat. 'I didn't intend the police to . . .' Before he could finish the sentence his eyes glazed and his mouth froze in a rictus. He crashed to the floor, his lifeless arms flailing the carpet.

'Kelburn, you fool! You damn fool!'

Temple rushed forward. He knelt beside the prostrate form, automatically putting a finger in Kelburn's mouth to make sure the breathing passage was clear. But Temple knew it was hopeless. He was straightening up when Raine, without knocking, walked into the cabin.

'Mr Temple, we've taken Mrs . . .' He stopped short when he saw the body. 'What it is? What's happened to Kelburn?'

Temple slowly got to his feet.

'He's dead, Raine.'

'What puzzles me,' said Raine, 'is why a man in his position should turn to crime.'

Forbes, Raine, Steve and Temple were seated round a table in the Meridian Bar of the liner. It was crowded with merrymaking passengers celebrating the first hours of the cruise to the Caribbean. Twenty minutes had passed since George Kelburn had taken the last escape route open to him. Laura Kelburn, to whom the news had been broken by Sir Graham, was in the sick bay being attended to by the ship's doctor, under the discreet surveillance of a police officer.

'It's a fallacy that big businessmen have no time for any other activities, Superintendent.' Temple had knocked back his first Scotch neat and was now drinking a second whisky diluted with soda. 'You've only to read the gossip columns to appreciate that.'

Raine smiled, taking the point. Forbes, cupping a balloon brandy glass in his hand, said: 'Yes, but why crime?'

'I don't suppose we'll ever know the full answer to that. There may even be more than one. But you have to admit the idea of a big-time fence operating on an international scale is a tempting one. Carried to its furthermost limits a man like that could become extremely powerful. And there's no doubt that Kelburn was obsessed with power.'

Steve had felt a faint tremor beneath her feet. Through the windows she could see the quayside cranes slipping past. 'Paul! I think the ship's moving!'

'I agree that's a fair estimate of the general picture,' Raine said, ignoring her comment. 'Now, let's get down to details. Who exactly was in this organisation?'

'We may never know the full extent of the organisation. Mike Langdon, Dr Benkaray and Larry Cross were certainly his chief lieutenants, and there were several smaller fry like Ted Angus, Oscar at the pet shop, Mrs Fletcher and Julia Kelburn.'

'His own daughter!' Steve's surprise had distracted her from the problem of how they were to get ashore.

'Yes, Steve. That's why he resented her friendship with Tony Wyman. He thought that Wyman might find out that she was working for The Fence – which is exactly what happened, of course. Wyman tried to get in on the easy money and found himself out of his depth.'

'But surely Kelburn's troubles started when he allowed Benkaray to persuade him that the biggest money lay in smuggling drugs?'

'That's true, Steve. His own daughter became an addict. Langdon had been against the drug activities right from the start, and Kelburn turned to him to try and get Julia out of the habit. But by this time Benkaray had realised that Julia was Kelburn's weak spot.'

Raine finished his drink and signalled the steward for a refill. 'You think Benkaray wanted to gain control of the organisation, then?'

'Everything points that way. Kelburn had built up the organisation and of course he resented anybody taking it over. At first, he didn't oppose her openly; in fact, he gave them a bigger cut in the profits to keep them quiet.'

'Them?' Forbes said. 'I take it Larry Cross was on Benkaray's side?'

'Naturally. However, one condition of the extra cut was that the doctor should stop supplying Julia with heroin. This drove Julia frantic. She made a special visit to Westerton to see the doctor, and on her father's instructions Mike

Langdon went to fetch her back. She became hysterical and threatened to tell all she knew. Langdon guessed she had already talked to Tony Wyman. He was badly rattled and when she openly defied him he lost control of himself and strangled her.'

'And Wyman, of course, was to be the suspect?'

'Yes. Kelburn saw to that.'

'But what was Wyman doing at Breakwater House?'

'He'd been tricked into going there, Sir Graham, just as Steve and I were lured there by that message from the girl, Fiona Scott. Wyman had been told to meet Kelburn at Breakwater House at the same time that Steve and I were due there.'

The beat of the engines quickened. The *Wyoming* was proceeding majestically down Southampton Water, a floating palace with all its pennants flying. Steve tried again to catch Paul's eye.

'Then what about the murder of Ted Angus?' Raine persisted.

'That's harder to account for. But my guess is that after he had failed to kill Tony Wyman, Dr Benkaray decided he was now useless and had served his purpose.'

A steward who had brought Raine a fresh pint of beer glanced enquiringly at Steve, with a murmured, 'Madam?' Steve nodded and he took away her empty glass. Through the windows of the bar she could see the lights on the Hampshire coast slipping past.

'Paul, how are we going to—'

But Forbes was still puzzled about the details and overrode her question. 'Temple, what did Angus mean when he told you to ask Mrs Fletcher about the coat?'

'He was referring to the coat worn by Julia Kelburn. This coat had the name Margo on it. Julia stole the coat and made arrangements to go to Brighton to see the fortune teller. She was hoping to exchange it for another coat containing a supply of heroin.'

'Do you think Langdon had any design on Kelburn's position?' asked Forbes.

'No, Sir Graham. I don't think so. Langdon was a typical executive, not a leader. Kelburn depended on him for the unpleasant jobs.'

'Then that nonsense about you having to watch Laura Kelburn was a sort of diversion,' Steve said angrily, 'a deliberate attempt to take you away from the main issue?'

'No, not entirely, Steve. Laura had been seeing Larry Cross and Kelburn was afraid she would tell Cross about his contacts and methods of working. It was Kelburn's practice to keep all this to himself as much as possible. Even his wife knew very little about it.'

'She's not the only wife to be kept in the dark,' Steve pointed out briskly. 'This ship sailed five minutes ago and here you men are, talking away as if we were in a pub in Southampton! Who's going to take me home?'

'I've arranged for a launch to come out from Gosport and take us off when we reach the end of Southampton Water,' Raine explained. 'There will be plenty of room for you and Mr Temple – as well as Laura Kelburn.'

Forbes cleared his throat. 'That may not be necessary.'

'What do you mean?' demanded Steve.

Forbes and Temple exchanged a smile. Even the phlegmatic Raine had caught the mood and was grinning.

'I believe you said you very much wanted to visit Jamaica, Steve,' said Forbes. 'Well, there's a verandah cabin on this ship which is now unoccupied. What's more, it has already been paid for. I've spoken to the Purser and he assures me . . .'

'But we haven't any . . .' Steve began. Then she suddenly smiled and, jumping up from her chair, kissed Sir Graham on the cheek. 'Sir Graham, you're a darling! This means Paul will have to buy me a completely new wardrobe!'

'By Timothy!' exclaimed Temple.

To everyone's surprise the Superintendent burst out laughing. 'That's one thing even *you* overlooked, Mr Temple,' said Raine.